DETROIT PUBLIC LIBRARY

CHILDREN'S LIBRARY
5201 Woodward
Detroit, MI 48202

DATE DUE

SONGBERD'S GROVE

Other books by ANNE BARRETT:

THE JOURNEY OF JOHNNY REW

THE DARK ISLAND

STOLEN SUMMER

CATERPILLAR HALL

SONGBERD'S GROVE

BY *Anne Barrett*

ILLUSTRATED BY N. M. BODECKER

THE BOBBS-MERRILL COMPANY · INC.

INDIANAPOLIS NEW YORK

J c.1

COPYRIGHT © 1957 BY ANNE MAINWARING BARRETT

PRINTED IN THE UNITED STATES OF AMERICA

LIBRARY OF CONGRESS CATALOG CARD NUMBER: 57-12852

M.J

PORTRAITS

Facing page

Mr. Triplett 15

The Intruder 38

No. 1 55

La Golondrina 78

The Face 99

The Height of Elegance 121

J. P. 144

The New Girl 161

Lord Simon Vigo 191

Her Own Level 243

SONGBERD'S GROVE

CHAPTER

1

"HERE?" said Martin. He sat bolt upright with shock and his round glasses seemed to bulge out in disbelief.

Mrs. Singer, his mother, looked distractedly into the holdall in her lap and then fished wildly into the two bursting carrier-bags beneath her arm. Finally she pulled up her handbag from where it had slipped down into the crack between her own and the driver's seat. She took out a dog-eared bit of paper and peered doubtfully down at the address which was written on it; but by this time the driver of the removal van had pulled up in front of a house.

"There you are then," he said. "No. 7 Songberd's Grove. Give us the word when you wants me and my mate to start unloading." And, lighting a cigarette, he jerked his head towards the man sitting amongst all the Singer household goods behind them.

"But this can't be it? The name . . ." Martin usually made it a point of honour to suppress all feelings in public, but his present agitation was driven out of him. "Songbirds . . . a grove. . . . A grove means trees." He turned his glass stare towards the driver as though to correct his ignorance.

"Not in London it don't, son. This is the place all right."

"It is, dear." Mrs. Singer, even shorter-sighted than her son, had finally satisfied herself that the address on her piece of paper and the name which was written over the row of houses matched. "No. 7 Songberd's Grove—and spelt wrong too, just as it was when the Housing Officer sent it to us. You really would think they'd know better in London, wouldn't you? 'Ring at the bell marked Triplett and ask for the key of the ground-floor flat.' Oh dear, I do hope it will be a nice place inside!"

Fumbling at all the leather and string and cardboard handles which she had to gather up and carry, Mrs. Singer let her mind wander off into a hopeful maze of possible rooms, cookers and sinks. Martin, gripping the side of the van till his knuckles shone, stared down at them in a moment of blank dismay.

He had to take one picture right out of his mind and put in another. As though it were a castle of bricks which he had carefully built and which someone had just kicked down, the Songberd's Grove of his imagination seemed to be falling all around him, golden bricks painted with dark leaves and bright feathers, gleaming as they turned in the air and fell clack to the ground. And in their place he had to put this. Reluctantly he looked up.

The block of seven blackish-grey houses was set back from the road, with their own pavement and an expanse of muddy earth, which had once been a private carriage-drive, in front of them, ending with a straggling privet hedge that ran along the real road's pavement. There were the remains of some things that had once been trees inside the hedge, with a litter of rubbish and broken milk bottles at their feet. Martin turned his eyes away quickly and looked at the actual fronts of the houses.

They were very old and not very high. A knowledgeable eye might have recognised and saluted the beauty of line and design that lay hidden behind their dirt and dilapidation. To Martin they looked like nothing so much as a collection of grimy old black-clothed women all huddled together: their toothless mouths the uncurtained windows, the sagging, uneven roofs their battered hats.

"Come on, love," said Mrs. Singer, descending with difficulty because of her many bundles, and difficult to understand because she had even to hold some of the more precious bits of paper between her teeth for safekeeping. "We want to get straight before your father comes. To think that we've got a place of our own at last!" And, picking up the parcels which had been allotted to him, Martin followed her down from the high driver's-cabin and on to the road.

To his horror, he saw that on either side of him, lined up all the way to the front door as though he were a bride going into the church, there were two lines of children, gazing at him with enormous concentration and in complete silence. Clutching his parcels to him and glaring at them from behind the blinding shields of his glasses, on which the afternoon sun was now shining, Martin strode past them and up to the front door. His mother had already rung the appropriate bell. The paint had once been red but was now darkened and peeling; there was a fanlight above with the number seven painted on it in black, with a thin gold edge. For the first time a touch of sympathy with the house stirred in Martin. It was a good seven.

Footsteps sounded from inside and an old man, frail and pinkish, stood blinking in front of them, as though he had suddenly been recalled from very far away. He was in his shirt-sleeves and slippers and wore a curious sort of tapestry waistcoat, from whose pocket the end of a tape measure was trailing. All over him, as though he had been sleeping inside a mattress, small bits of cloth and thread and horsehair were clinging, and a pad stuck full of pins was attached to one of his wrists.

"Ah, you'll be the new tenants, I expect?" The old tailor gave them an uncertain wavering smile as he looked over the top of his half-moon glasses at them. And as he stood back to let them in he seemed to be as insubstantial as one of his own wisps of cotton.

"The three rooms along this side are your place." He gestured vaguely. "Bathroom and such, which we share, along under the stairs here, and my little room beyond." As he mentioned the stairs, Martin looked upwards and was conscious of a sudden withdrawal from above, as though someone had been peering down through the bannisters which wound dimly away over his head. At the same time he suddenly became aware of a variety of cooking smells: an honest, straight-forward one seeping out from Mr. Triplett's room and a strange, oily, spicy one coming down from above.

Seeing his quivering nostrils, the old man seemed to come fully alive at last. He gave him the ghost of a wink and the ghost of a smile.

Mr. Triplett

"Smelling my supper, eh?" he asked. "Onions!" And he jerked his head sideways in satisfaction. "Bit of steak to 'em, too, tonight," he added, to Martin's surprise, for it seemed to him altogether too strong a diet for such a wispy man. "Yes, we get to know each other's tastes and fancies here all right. Still, it's not such a bad place as they go, and we're lucky to have anywhere of our own, the way things are nowadays. You been on the list a long time, Missis?"

Mrs. Singer nodded. For seven years, ever since Martin's father had been moved up to work in London, they had been living apart from him, seeing him only at week-ends.

"Flat above's empty too," said Mr. Triplett, who was talking quite easily now, as though he had only needed warming up and had now got back into the way of it. "They say the folks is coming in next week. I hope they'll be decent and not like some of the trash we've got here. Well, I mustn't stand here talking. I expect you'll be wanting to move in and see your place now." And he held out the key. "I'm down there, like I told you, if you should want anything." He gestured down beyond the stairs to where a long, grey-filmed window seemed to give onto something that might be a garden. Mrs. Singer clucked her tongue in disapproval as she looked at it, shifted all her parcels under one arm to take the key in the other hand and thought longingly of a big bowl of soap and water and a chamois leather.

" 'Tain't a bad place," repeated the old man, moving towards his own room and looking over his shoulder at Martin, "but from what I sees and hears I should say you want to go carefully, son." And with this final and ominous pronouncement he disappeared inside. Martin took his wondering gaze away from him and brought his attention back to the business on hand.

"Here, love, while I open the door." Mrs. Singer piled a few more carriers on top of the parcels that he already held, so that at first he could see nothing but a wall of brown paper as he staggered in after her. Then one by one, as though he had been buried under a pile of debris and she were slowly uncovering him, she plucked them off him again and he was free.

He saw that they were in the first of the three rooms, the kitchen, and that Mrs. Singer was already examining the stove with an expert eye.

"Not bad," she said, "though the sink's a small one. And there's a fireplace in here too! I reckon we'll sit in this room, it'll be cosy in the winter." And she looked with approval at the delicate little fireplace, with its carved marble mantelpiece. It had been left behind from the more spacious days when their entire flat had been only the drawing-room of the old house, and it seemed as out of place in its new setting as Cinderella's white foot beneath her dingy kitchen clothes.

Released from his parcels, Martin went on into the next room. It was nearly square and still had the ceiling rose that had once hung in the centre of the drawing-room, moulded with a pattern of vine leaves and grapes.

Once more, from behind him, as she looked at the festoons of cobwebs which the spiders had helpfully but mistakenly added to the decoration, Mrs. Singer clicked her tongue.

"Your father and I will sleep in here, I dare say," she said. "It's not a bad room either, though it is darkish. Funny to sleep on the ground floor with everyone in the street walking by." Rubbing her finger in passing on the little window that gave on to the street, for No. 7 was the end house of the block, she followed Martin in through the last door.

"And this one for you. Well, it certainly isn't a palace, but it's a roof of our own." After looking up for a moment at what was now their own ceiling, with all the pent-up relief that seven long years under a bad-tempered sister-in-law's roof had accumulated inside her, she hurried back through the two open doors to summon in the furniture men. Martin was left in his own domain.

DET·PUB·LIB

It was a queer, narrow slice of a room that at first seemed to be all window and door. It would be rather like living in a greenhouse, he thought, for at this moment all the evening sun was streaming in. In front of him, as he stood in the doorway, was a long, arched window that came down to the ground and opened out in two halves on to a little balcony—the twin in shape to the long window at the end of the passage, and the twin in dirtiness too. To his left there was a small window looking out on to the street, as in his parents' room, and to his right, in the corner of the opposite wall, a door out into the passage. That was a good thing—it meant he had his own private entrance and would not have to come through his parents' room every time.

He stepped across to the long window and opened the catch. Streamers of black cobweb fluttered away from his fingers as the two doors swung open, and he wiped them on his trousers absent-mindedly. There was a small openwork iron platform outside, pierced with a pattern of scrolls and stars, and then three steps leading down into the narrow strip of rubbly garden. Stepping out on to it cautiously, he saw that Mr. Triplett seemed to have the same sort of balcony on the other side; he could hear the whirring of a sewing-machine, punctuated by the occasional snip of scissors.

He wasn't going to venture out into the garden for the moment, for the watching eyes might be looking down at him from windows all round, and he wanted to do some thinking before he showed himself to them again. He felt as though he were the first person to land on the shores of a new planet and that its unknown, peculiar inhabitants were watching from behind every stone. He went inside again to consider his position.

A couple of chairs had somehow found their way through the door, pushed out by the general turmoil that was going on in the other two rooms. He sat down on one of them and rested his chin on the back of the other. The recent events of his life still seemed to be whirling round him like the settling colours in a kaleidoscope, and he wasn't yet used to the new pattern.

With difficulty he thought back to this morning, the last one after seven years in his aunt's house. The day and the miles between had spun away so fast that now he could hardly even visualise the prim little house in a row of others exactly like it; the two bow windows and the two neat rose-trees; the bare, square garden with no dark or secret places. "Emandalf"; his Uncle Alfred's and his Aunt Emmeline's first names had been joined together to christen the house in the only original or dashing gesture they had ever made. It was the unpleasantly uneven, misshapen letters painted on the gate by Uncle Alf that, by their very wrongness, had first made Martin realise his feeling for letters and numbers. He sighed.

And now there was Songberd's Grove. Ever since he had first heard about it, he had lain awake night after night with excitement and thought about it, in the small and box-like room at the top of Emandalf which he had somehow managed to stamp with his own personality. The letter saying that they had been allotted a flat had come one morning at breakfast, and as soon as he heard the name a picture of tall, swaying tree trunks, dark leaves and brilliant songbirds had rushed into his mind and stayed there ever since. The outer suburbs had so far been his only experience of life; he knew nothing about either London or country and, imagining the same elements of mystery and excitement into both, had grown rather confused. Except to think that his father was going to come home every night now, that his mother would be able to cook as she liked and that Aunt Emmeline would no longer be able to chase round after him with damp cloths and dusters, he did not bother to think about it in any more detail.

Batty. That's what he was. He made a face to express his self-scorn, shook his head to blow away the past and got down to grips with reality. He looked round his room, and suddenly, as though out of a richness of old experience, the room seemed to wink and chuckle back at him. Martin sat upright and blinked behind his glasses. This wasn't just a bit of space, like the rooms at Emandalf, but a place with character; it had a personality just as strong as his own. Who had lived here? He had never met anywhere like this before. He stared round it for a minute and then slowly grinned, as though he had met a new person that he liked.

He followed with his eyes the line of the moulding round the ceiling, and the border of vine leaves and grapes cut short by the new and dividing wall. He looked up and down the shapely windows and at the sturdy brass catches which fastened them.

He would have the bed along the inner wall, he thought, with its head so he could look out of the window; put something to hang his clothes on on the wall opposite the window, by the door in the partition. Work-table just to one side of the big window so that the latter could still be opened and used to go down into the garden below. He nodded, and had not decided a moment too soon, for the other two rooms were settled now and the remaining tide of objects came washing into his.

A rug was unrolled and the bed was brought in; the van man and his mate came staggering with the solid wooden table which was Martin's pride and joy. Obeying the boy's authoritatively pointing finger he dumped it down in the chosen spot, to one side of the long window, and as he backed out again Martin's mother came in with a brush and her long-desired bowl of soapy water.

From beyond the two open doors Martin could see flames that crackled and shot tongues of brightness from the kitchen fireplace, and the smell of wood-smoke came wafting through them. His mother had wasted no time; in No. 7 Songberd's Grove, for better or worse, the Singer family was now at home.

CHAPTER

2

At half-past six Mr. Singer got back from the engineering works where he was a draughtsman, gave a doubtful look at the outside of Songberd's Grove and rang his own doorbell. Martin opened the door, but before he got caught up in the rush of welcome to his father he was aware once more of movements and watchers outside and quick withdrawals into other doorways. Feeling as though he were pulling up the drawbridge of a besieged fortress, he drew his father in quickly and across the hall into the safety of their own room.

"Well!" said Mr. Singer and rubbed his hands. A large fire was now crackling away in the elegant fireplace, for although it was summer, Mrs. Singer had wanted to disperse the musty, unused atmosphere of the rooms, and to air out their chairs and sofa which had been so long in store. She had found a blue-checked cloth from somewhere among the luggage, and on the table which this now adorned, pilchards, tomatoes and a new loaf of bread were spread out.

"The old things, eh?" Her husband looked around the room with satisfaction and then sank down comfortably into the dent in the old sofa which he had made a long time ago, before the war. "Sorry I couldn't get over to clean it up a bit for you, but I've been working overtime. They delivered the wood and coal all right, I see. It's not much of a place outside, I'm afraid, but this is a bit of all right!" He looked round the friendly room once again and lit his pipe.

"It's all right, love," said Mrs. Singer, giving him a pat on the knee as she passed, "though it's shocking dirty." Happiness and relief at being in her own place and away from her sister-in-law had made her fluff out and glow like a wet hen that had just been dried off in front of a fire, but at the moment she was preoccupied, searching again for something elusive in her bag.

"I do believe I've gone and lost the key of the suitcase that's got the aired sheets in it. Run out, Martin, and see if I dropped it outside in the fuss of coming in. A little silly key, you know the one." And the thing that Martin dreaded had come upon him. Like the newly arrived voyager to the moon that he imagined himself to be, he had to step out of the security of his space-ship and tread on the unknown territory; the things that lurked behind the trees and the stones of the moonscape or, in other words, behind the pillars and doorways of Songberd's Grove, would be able to get him. Squaring his shoulders and whistling a little, settling his glasses firmly in their place, he moved away from the safe Singer territory and out of the door.

The low sun was slanting across the trodden mud waste in front of the houses and turned them into a sort of Sahara Desert, in which the shallow pools that were left from yesterday's rain gleamed like pieces of metal. Martin blinked for a moment in the orange glow and then was aware once more of the silent, watching children.

"Hallo, kids," he said jauntily, but there was no reply, except for a faint giggle that ran through them like the wind through barley. Only the younger ones seemed to be out at this moment. Turning his back on them, Martin started to examine the ground in front of No. 7 systematically, kicking the little pool in each depression with his toecap till the water spurted up, but he could find no key. Well, it wasn't here; they would just have to break open the suitcase, that was all. He straightened and half-turned to go in again when he was aware that two larger boys had come up behind him, as silently as though they had been playing grandmother's steps, or like two greased natives through the jungle.

One of them, who had muddy-coloured hair and a muddy-coloured face to match, and light, expressionless eyes the colour of dirty bath-water, handed him a bit of paper. The other was rusty-haired and heavily freckled, with bright blue eyes. He wore a blue and white striped tee-shirt and he looked nervous and rather cowed. Martin stared at them.

"Message from No. 1," said Mudface shortly. "Wants to see you tomorrow, nine-thirty sharp."

Still Martin looked at them, from the bottom step of No. 7, and realised now that the small fry had come back again and were grouped about behind the two larger ones, listening with interest. The fact that he was on his own doorstep gave him courage.

"Who's No. 1?" he asked, in his most off-hand voice, "I don't know that I particularly want to see him." And as he gazed down loftily into Mudface's eyes the small crowd behind him gasped.

"No. 1 lives in No. 1 and he's called No. 1 because he is No. 1!" said Mudface fiercely, all on one tone, as though repeating a lesson. "And you'd better come!" Turning on his heel he grabbed the rusty one and marched away. It seemed to Martin that the latter gave him a fleeting look of interest and almost of sympathy as he went, leaving Martin and the curious crowd to stare at one another.

"Good night," he said casually, as he mounted the last step, and as though his defiance had given them courage, a faint, uncertain answering murmur came from one or two of his watchers. He closed the front door behind him and leant against it for a moment inside. He had a strong feeling that somehow and somewhere war had been declared.

"Found it, love!" said his mother, flushed and beaming, as he went in, for her husband had just given her a smacking kiss. She held the key up in one hand and all the aired and home-smelling sheets over the other arm. "Sorry to have sent you out on a fool's errand, but there, I expect you've been getting to know some of the others and seen a likely friend or two. Supper's ready when I've put these down."

With a look of affectionate pity at her total, grown-up lack of comprehension, Martin smoothed down his hair again and slipped the piece of paper into his pocket; then he went over to the table and sat down. It was a leisurely, pleasant meal. Some time later they were all still sitting in the gloaming, relishing the fact of being round their own table and relaxing in the broad glow of the fire, which now winked on the knife blades and on the silvery skins of the remaining pilchards, flickering over the white bread and yellow butter and the bright, exciting red of the tomato sauce.

"Well, Bedfordshire!" said Mrs. Singer, leaning back in her chair so that the firelight found a new surface, the starched white of tablecloth and of her clean apron, to wander on. In her contentment and peace at being at home again she had wandered back a few years, remembering the old words that she had used in those early days and forgetting Martin's age. Although it was a point that he would normally have taken up with her, tonight he was not reluctant to go to bed; he wanted some privacy to look at the note which No. 1 had sent him and to consider the situation in which he found himself. He also wanted to find out more about his new and curiously strong-charactered room.

"Going to try our new bathroom? I've cleaned it up a bit." Martin shook his head vigorously. Last night he had scrubbed himself meticulously, every inch of his body, and even washed his hair, in a sort of symbolic cleansing to show that he had washed all of Emandalf away. That ought to last well into tomorrow, if not longer, and he didn't want to risk the passage, and the watching eyes above it, for a minute longer than he need tonight.

"All right, do your teeth and your face in the sink here tonight then, but don't think you're going to make a habit of it!" And going off to make his bed while he did so, Mrs. Singer came back to bid him a cheerful good-night and, wanting to talk to her husband, despatched him through the two doors and into solitude.

The dim evening light in his room was rather fascinating as Martin went to the window and looked out. It softened and rounded the large chunks of stone among the rubble in the garden till they seemed to be made of some finer, more noble substance, and lit up the few weeds that struggled up amongst them to a vivid green; it was not light enough, however, to read his note. He switched on the naked bulb that hung from the ceiling and instantly the garden just outside was marked out in sharp edges and deep shadows. He sat down in the chair by his work table and unfolded the note, the familiar and friendly grain of the wood in front of him seemed to give him support.

Report to No. 1 Songberd's Grove 9:30 a.m. tomorrow, it said, and nothing more, except that underneath it was written a one or an I—a large, clumsy, wobbling letter that excited Martin's deepest disgust.

If he hadn't been decided before, that would have settled it. To be ordered about by anybody was not his idea at all, but to be ordered about by somebody who didn't know any better than to make letters like that! Getting out his favourite stump of pencil from his pocket, Martin tentatively drew another one beside it; straight, shapely and self-respecting. He outlined it firmly, shaded it to give it thickness and then, having put his own mark of defiance on the letter, crossed the other one out, screwed the paper up in a ball and threw it down on the floor.

Another thought came to him and with a deep sigh he recognized it for what it was. It came from the troublesome inner man he possessed, who was apt to speak up and dictate to him at unexpected moments, nearly always uncomfortably. Let someone else dare you to do something and you could do it or not as you chose—it was even a peculiar sort of courage, he had found out, to let them think you a coward when you weren't. Dare yourself, however, with these tiresome inner dares that came from goodness knows where, and you had to do it. This was one of those. He knew that he had to take up the letter, uncrumple it, and lay it now, with his own mark upon it, on the doorstep of No. 1. It was a pity; he would have liked more time to think out some plan of action, but there it was—he knew it had to be done.

He stuck his head through the passage door of the fire-lit sitting-room, and his father, with his arm round his mother's shoulders, turned to look.

"Just going out to get a good-night breath of air," Martin said. "Once round the block." Waving far more airily than his feeling justified, he left the door of No. 7 ajar and stepped outside.

In the time that it had taken him to draw his defiant letter, the light had gone. It was dark now and the street lamps gleamed on the top leaves of the privet hedge. The mud flat was chequered with varying squares of light as some of the ground-floor windows were curtained and some were not; some people had even turned out their lights altogether and gone to bed. The same had happened in the first-floor flats, merely flinging the chequers of light farther out.

What should he do? In the darkness of the doorway Martin considered. Dodge across the black squares, like a chessman? But even as he watched them they changed, a light flicking on here, flicking off there; he might suddenly find himself completely flood-lit. Take the safe way, right round the outer edge of the hedge and in at the other end for No. 1? But the wretched dare that had started up in his mind was still going on at him. The most direct way, it said; begin as you mean to go on. Under the windows? So close that anyone looking out could even recognise his face as he passed?

Taking a deep breath Martin had started even before he was aware of it, like someone who has got to get it over diving suddenly into an ice-cold sea. With his head down and not looking at the uncovered windows he tore down past the first few houses, but the tiresome creature inside him was still not satisfied. "What about the Charge of the Light Brigade?" it said scornfully. "Did they gallop? No, they trotted; anyone can do things in a rush." And so, at No. 4, Martin slowed down, raised his head and stared defiantly in. The colourless eyes of Mudface met his for a moment, and Martin saw him jump to his feet. He walked past, deposited his note, weighted down with a stone, on the doorstep of No. 1 and then started back.

The door of No. 2 didn't open and no one came out, but just as he passed it and was steeling himself for No. 4 a window was flung up above him and something flashed out. Like a bird which suddenly senses danger behind it, Martin put on an extra spurt and dashed just out of reach of the bucketful of water that splashed down behind him. So breathless that it hurt him he squeezed in through their own door and banged it shut behind him.

"That was a short turn," said his father. Grinning

feebly, without enough breath to speak, Martin nodded and went back to his room. Honour was avenged and he was at peace for the moment. To-morrow must take care of itself.

CHAPTER

3

MARTIN UNPACKED his suitcase with great care. Clothes were not particularly important, and there was nowhere to hang them yet anyway. His father was going to put up a row of hooks for him and would try and find him a second-hand chest of drawers tomorrow. In the meantime he humped them all out onto the spare chair until it began to look like a small elephant. But at the bottom of the suitcase were the really important things—his lettering books, his inks and his cards of special pen nibs, the chisel and small hammer which the old stonemason in his yard at Babbler's Green had given him.

There were only two things that Martin regretted about leaving Emandalf. One was Rufus, the mongrel dog from the shop whom he used to take walks, and the other was Mr. Acle and his stonemason's yard, to which Rufus, in a wild and glorious cat chase one day had led him. As Martin had stood awkwardly among the strange litter of marble blocks and figures, apologising, he had looked around him with curiosity. There were groups for public fountains, bird-baths and horses' drinking-troughs. Lying carelessly about on the grass, between chips of stone and marble, were bright new headstones and weeping angels, awaiting their reluctant customers. Beneath them all were cut suitable inscriptions, and it was these that really held Martin's attention. These were what letters should be! He felt round one with his finger, and, seeing the old stonemason's eyes upon him, tried to explain about the wrongness of the letters at Emandalf.

"Ah," said Mr. Acle, "that gate. Yes, I seen it. Can't treat letters like that, you got to give them room." And he then and there proceeded, in the loose earth at his feet, to rough out the letters of Emandalf as they should have been, discoursing on the amount of space needed by E's and L's and the leggy awkwardness of M's and N's, to Martin's fascination.

"See?" he said. "Have a go." And he handed Martin the stick he had been using. "Silly name that is, write your own." And as Martin drew down the first strokes of his M, their friendship began.

Well, he would have to do all these things on his own now. He picked out the few odd-shaped bits of stone that he had fancied and brought to practise on and laid them out on the table. Mr. Acle had said that he would pick him out some larger ones when he had learnt a bit more, but what was the good of that now? His eye lit on the garden and he brightened. Plenty of stone out there, if only it were the right sort. But the sight of the garden brought his mind back to the present and difficult times.

Well, there wasn't much he could do at the moment, not until he knew what No. 1 was like and what would happen when he didn't obey the silly summons. Better to sleep on it. He opened the long window and then got in between the clean sheets. His own bed out of store was much softer and more friendly than any of Aunt Emmeline's well-stuffed ones had been; the very lumps seemed to be Singer lumps and he liked them. He sniffed appreciatively at the different smell of their own linen. Suddenly he was very sleepy, almost dizzy with it, in fact. The bed seemed to sway beneath him as if it were the jolting removal van in which they had travelled up from Babbler's Green. For a drowsy moment he watched a small spider that hung down from the electric light bulb and seemed to be swinging in the same rhythm as the bed, then he turned up the switch beside him and was instantly asleep.

But the early bedtime had upset his pattern of sleeping. Quite suddenly, in the middle of the night, he found himself fully awake, with the black and silver moonlight, that turned everything to corners, flooding in. His room was mostly corners, anyway; from the deep warmth and luxury of a bed from which he didn't have to get up, he considered it. Corners of walls and corners of doors and shutters, corners of ceilings and of the moulding which went in a wide band round it, the flowing pattern of vine leaves and grapes picked out and shaded by the moonlight.

He was lying contentedly on his back, looking up through the arch of the window at the bright, thin moon, which he could just see, when suddenly, from the top of the window, a dark line, like the thread of the spider, appeared.

Could it be another, a huge one, outside? In the still, fantastic moonlight, and at this queer hour, almost anything seemed possible. The line lengthened, blackened and became thicker, swayed for a moment or two across a segment of the window and then settled to cross it in an oblique line down to the floor of his balcony. It was the iron ladder of an ancient fire escape which had been lowered.

Fully alert now, Martin shrank back against the wall by his bed and put on his glasses. Loosening the bedclothes so that he could jump out in a minute if necessary, he clutched his long torch which had a usefully heavy head. Weren't they even going to leave him alone at night-time? He waited.

The iron ladder quivered a little and then sagged under a weight; somebody was coming down it. A shapeless overboot appeared and then another; trou-sered legs above them bent and straightened cautiously as the feet felt for one rung after another. Whoever it was might have a torch to shine in, thought Martin; he would be safer at the foot of his bed, by the window. Quickly and silently, before the head and shoulders appeared, he had slid down there and stepped out of bed, flattened against the wall.

Hands came now and sleeves, and something dark that flapped above them. In spite of his tension, Martin was filled with scorn. Good heavens! A shawl! What a thing to wind round your head on an expedition like this. Then the figure's first foot had touched the ground and any time for wondering was over.

It crouched for a moment at the foot of the ladder,

The Intruder

and then quickly, and with only a fleeting look into Martin's room, made off down the balcony steps and into the garden. What could they want there? Stones? Was the chap going to get some ammunition? Tightening his grip on the torch, Martin slid out round the open window and stood in the shadowed darkness by the foot of the ladder; the moment to get him would be on his way back, when he was looking into the room.

The figure, still bent and stooping, was picking up something from the ground. It straightened, and Martin had only a moment to wonder at its smallness before it was running up the steps again. With one hand and one foot on the ladder, still not having seen him, it paused for a moment, peering curiously into his room, the other hand loaded, as he supposed, and hanging ready down to one side. It lifted the hand.

"No, you don't!" said Martin and jabbed at it with his torch. He quickly stepped forward at the same time to fling his other arm across the ladder and stop it going up.

There was a small cry and the hand that he had hit dropped down again and opened; nothing hard fell out of it but only something that looked like a squashed lump of leaves and grass. In a sudden swift movement the shawled head bent down and he felt a quick pain on the back of his hand on the ladder.

It had bitten him! In his surprise, he drew it away, and then, as he moved back, furious with himself, the creature's other hand gave him a stinging smack on the face and something black, woolly and smothering descended all round his head and blinded him. The shawl! He struggled with it wildly, caught his glasses in it as he dragged it off and had to fumble to stick them on again before he could see anything properly; by which time the figure had gone and the end of the fire escape was rising above his head.

He gave a wild jump and just touched it with his fingers before it was jerked upwards and slid out of reach. He heard a window shut quickly and nothing but calm moonlight filled the tranquil garden again.

Stinging with the smart of the bite and the worse smart of indignity of allowing himself to be smothered in a shawl and made ridiculous, Martin bunched up the woollen cloth and threw it down disgustedly while he bent to see what had been dropped with the bundle of grass on the balcony. Perhaps another of their silly notes. Or was this a rival gang? Oddly enough, there seemed to be nothing there but leaves and some small, pale, spicy-smelling flowers. Puzzled, he laid them all out on his desk. Life at Songberd's Grove seemed to be becoming more complicated every moment. But there was still No. 1 to be dealt with tomorrow and now he felt he needed sleep. He looked undecidedly at the shutters for a moment and then pushed the windows wide open again. To shut them now would be a confession of defeat. Anyway, he had a strong feeling that no one would disturb him again tonight.

CHAPTER

4

In the light of the bright, cheerful morning to which Martin woke, the excitements of the strange evening and night before seemed as far-off and improbable as if he had dreamt them. The side of his room by the bed was flecked with sunlight, dancing like a handful of scattered golden coins on the wall, and the air which came in through the long window was fresh and exhilarating. The room itself seemed to greet him with a further degree of friendship, as though it was getting as used to him as he to it. But, to remind him that everything was not as innocent and straightforward as it appeared, the bunch of withered green stuff still lay on the table.

As he went out into the sun-dappled passage on his way to wash his face, Martin was greeted by the old tailor coming back from the front door with his paper and a bottle of milk; when he emerged from the bathroom a few minutes later, a delicious smell of breakfast came out from his own family's sitting-room, together with a clatter of crockery and the sound of his parents' cheerful voices.

As always during the first few days in a new place, there was a feeling of picnic in the air. Last night the table with their supper on it had been the main focus of the room, and the rest had withdrawn into the shadows, but now the stacks of household goods waiting to be sorted and the grimy, cobwebby corners to which Mrs. Singer had not yet had time to penetrate became apparent. Martin foresaw a busy day and sighed. He had problems enough of his own on his mind, but saw no chance at the moment of getting time to think them out.

All the same, after the silent, disapproving breakfasts at Aunt Emmeline's, it was very pleasant to be sitting at ease in their own room. His father and mother were discussing their plans for the day.

"I dare say I'll be able to get off a bit early," Mr. Singer was saying. "Back before five if I'm lucky through the traffic with my bike. If you and young

Martin can have got straight by then, we'll all three of us go off on a spending spree and look for the few more sticks of furniture we want. Chest of drawers for his room and somewhere to hang his clothes; a couple more chairs for this room, nice bit of fancy mirror to go over the fireplace, and perhaps a plant in a pot to go in front of it."

He looked at the clock. "Got to leave myself plenty of time to get there mornings, they're proper tartars on time. Gave a man the sack the other week because he'd been late three days running."

"That's all right, love," said Mrs. Singer. "We're good and early." The little mountains of scrambled egg that she put down in front of Martin and his father were a cheerful bright yellow and the toast beneath them lavishly buttered, as though in defiance of the absent and skimping Aunt Emmeline. She watched them eat for a moment and then, bringing over the fat, brown friendly teapot, that was to her the symbol of her new freedom and their newly regained family life, she stood happily for a few seconds with both hands cradled round it.

"We'll get it done all right, we've a fine day for it too. Where's the milk now, and the papers? Oh, I never brought them in. Get them for me, Martin, there's a good boy." And once again, by forces beyond his control, Martin was pushed out of his temporary security and brought face to face with his problems.

Not that he really expected anything to happen yet—it was barely eight o'clock and the summons wasn't for until half-past nine. But all the same if they had spies above him and spies who peered down through the bannisters, spies who let themselves down like spiders in the middle of the night, he couldn't let himself relax for a minute. He was all for a quiet life himself, but if things like this were going to happen they had to be dealt with. He pushed back his chair, and, whistling with elaborate nonchalance, went out of the front door.

He had been over-optimistic. Instead of having breakfast with their parents, as he had hoped, most of the children were already out; three of them in particular, Mudface, the small blue-eyed boy and another taller youth, were grouped near No. 7. They had evidently been told to change their tactics, for they bowed to him with mock politeness. He looked at them appraisingly from the top step and slightly inclined his head in return. Then he bent down to pick up the two milk bottles, but just before his hands got there he saw that there was a toecap just touching each one.

"Guess yer pa'd be cross without any milk to his tea," observed Mudface casually.

"Sure an' he's right," echoed Rusty rather pleadingly, in a husky Irish accent, and in the manner of one repeating a lesson.

"He'd be flipping cross if he had to mend a puncture and was late for work." The taller one, who had a particularly unpleasant voice and a flap of yellow hair falling over his forehead, was holding a nail in his hand and drawing it gently up and down one tyre of Mr. Singer's bicycle, which had been left padlocked to the railings outside No. 7.

An oldish man on his way to work came out of the door of No. 6, and for the moment that he was passing them the three boys relaxed and started laughing and talking gibberish, pretending that they were an ordinary group of friends. Trying to seize his opportunity, Martin bent swiftly towards the milk bottles, meaning to back quickly with them in his hands towards the bicycle, but the toes and the nail were there again before him.

"Martin!" His mother's voice came impatiently from the room behind him. Yielding to circumstances and to superior force, he looked at his three tormentors and raised his eyebrows in question.

"Well?" he said.

"Nine-thirty," said the long one.

Martin nodded. "All right. I'll come." And the threatening toecaps and the hand with the nail were withdrawn. As he turned up the steps to go in they sauntered away.

"Well, what a time just to get a bottle of milk!" said his mother, and again, under cover of his glasses, Martin looked at her with affectionate pity. Grown-ups! They made tea, poured milk into it and drank it; washed and cleaned up and spent their whole lives doing a hundred petty and unimportant things. And all the while, under their blind eyes, great battles were being fought out and issues settled. "You look sulky," they said, when your mind was seething with problems. "Run out and play," they said when the intricate solutions were first, faintly, beginning to dawn and you needed absolute stillness to concentrate on them. "Fetch in the milk, dear," and look what had nearly happened! Still, within their limited notions, they did their best, he supposed. So much to his mother's surprise that it nearly made her choke, he patted her briefly and absent-mindedly on the elbow before he went back to his rather cold scrambled egg. Quarter-past eight now and his interview was for half-past nine.

Mrs. Singer's own strategy for the house was rather like one of those games where you move letters and numbers up into little slots and others down again to take their place. She was going to move all the kitchen things into the bedroom while she cleaned the kitchen, all the bedroom things into Martin's room while she cleaned the bedroom, and the few objects from Martin's narrow strip of room out onto the balcony and into the passage while she had her final skirmish. The old man in the end room had been asked if he minded and had offered his help with the heavy things; in appreciation Mrs. Singer had asked him to come in and have a cup of tea with them in the evening, when the battle would be over. Today was going to be her supreme justification after the seven years with Aunt Emmeline and just for the moment she even welcomed the extreme dirt and squalor of Songberd's Grove because it made a more worthy obstacle against which to hurl her long pent-up house-pride and energy. With a flourish, almost as though she were blowing a trumpet, she lifted the first chair from the kitchen into the bedroom and battle was joined.

By nine-fifteen they had carried all the furniture out and the first room was empty; like tall, fantastically helmeted lieutenants Mrs. Singer and her brooms, mops and ceiling brushes were lined up by the door.

"You can go out for a bit now if you like," she said

to Martin. "Reckon it'll be dry enough to put the furniture back and go on to the next room in about an hour, so come back then."

Reluctantly, because he had somehow felt that as long as he was moving furniture he was safe, and now there was no excuse not to be getting ready, he went along to his room.

It was all right to make your mind up to do something—that was fairly easy—but how could you be sure that your body would obey? It was all right to decide on the sort of things that you were going to say, but how could you know what voice they would come out in?

As though it were a dog of whose training he wasn't quite sure, Martin looked down at his body, spreading out his hands in the sunlight, and besought it to do him credit. It was a good body, compact although slight, with light, strong bones and quick reactions. As he bent down to examine his hands, which somehow seemed to be its spokesmen, the sun glinted on his fine, fox-coloured hair and lit up the strange colour of his eyes behind his glasses.

He smoothed down his hair as flat as it would go and examined his finger nails. It seemed necessary to be as near perfection as he could make himself, in every respect. There were still five minutes to go; his eyes wandered round the room and he caught sight of the leaves and flowers, withered now, which he had laid out on his desk last night.

He smelt them again and felt bothered by them; they didn't make sense. All this business about No. 1 and Mudface seemed fairly obvious. He supposed that No. 1 was just some bully who had managed to get all the other children into his power and now wanted to get him, Martin, too—by what unpleasant methods it remained to be seen. Nearly every school playground had one of those. If whoever it was had thrown in a stone last night or tried to mess his room up, he would have understood better, but why just a handful of leaves? It was so futile. Remembering the shawl, he picked it up from where he had thrown it and spread it out; it was a foreign-looking sort of thing with a knotted fringe and a queer smell. Mr. Triplett had said that the flat above them was empty, so anyone might have got in there. Rolling it up again, he remembered that all his furniture was shortly going to be moved and he thrust it down inside his bed for safety.

Nine-twenty-five. This was it. Quickly, without giving himself time to think, with a last, silent appeal to his tight-strung and trembling body, he went out into the passage and opened the front door. From opposite the house, by the privet hedge, Mudface was watching impassively. Slowly and jauntily, with one hand in his pocket, past the little girls who were making mud castles in the roadway and the others who were sitting on the steps with their dolls, like a cock picking his way across a farmyard, Martin walked down the row.

Of all the blackened, decrepit and shame-faced houses, No. 1 was the worst. Nearly all the paint had been picked off the blistering doorway, and the black-out paint that had covered the fanlight during the war still remained there in streaks and patches, obliterating the number. Only a brass lion's-head knocker, like the one on the Singers' door, remained of the house's past substance, and that was green with verdigris. Without giving himself time to think, Martin took his hand out of his pocket quickly and banged it not only hard but seven times.

"Now then, softly, dearie!" To his utter astonishment the door was opened by the very opposite of what he had expected, a shapeless, floppy woman whose very essence seemed soft and stupid. She stood there in a grubby apron and carpet slippers and gave him a foolish and meaningless smile.

"Another o' Lennie's friends? Just along the passage there. I expect he'll have finished his breakfast by now; just bring the things out to me to wash, will you? I'm waiting to go out. He likes us to knock before we go in."

Martin stared at her in horror. Could this be Lennie's mother, waiting to wash his breakfast things instead of making him do his own, talking about knocking? He could just see his own parents! So his name was Lennie—no wonder he called himself something else! This flat was the other way round to the Singers' because it was the house at the other end of the row, and he moved on to where she pointed, to the door of the best room in the middle, the equivalent of his parents'. He looked back at her for a moment and then at the door. There was silence in the passage and silence in the room; evidently Lennie had heard his arrival and was waiting inside.

Moving very quickly, his inner man having suddenly taken control again, Martin wrenched the handle open without knocking and walked straight in.

"Hallo, Lennie," he said cheerfully, before he even looked up, and then stood blinking and with a ducked head, like someone who has just thrown a stone at a window and waits for the crash and shower of broken glass. But the silence, evidently copied from a tough film set-up and calculated to make him feel nervous, went on. As nothing happened, Martin looked up.

There were two boys in the room. At the back, in the shadows, stood the one with floppy hair, and in front of him, sitting back in an armchair behind a pushed-back breakfast tray, was Lennie or No. 1.

No. 1

He was an older boy than Martin or any of the others and much larger, with very broad shoulders and a shock of dark hair. He looked to Martin exactly like a bull in a field waiting to charge, and it seemed all the more extraordinary to see him sitting there, in pyjamas and dressing-gown, behind such a tray. Martin looked at it.

It was a startling meal for the slovenly woman outside to have produced. There had evidently been toast, bacon and grapefruit on it, and a small napkin was crumpled up at one side, beside a coffee-pot. Coffee! The Singers considered themselves lucky if they could afford it at Christmas. Martin now looked back with interest at Lennie's dressing-gown.

Silk! Cor, he really had been studying the films! Admittedly it was frayed at the collar and there was an untidy patch where a pocket or a monogram should have been, but it was silk for all that. Before he knew what he was doing Martin shook his head and clicked his tongue in a gesture of mock admiration.

"Stop that!" As No. 1 relapsed into poker-faced silence again, glaring at him, Martin was suddenly overcome by the supreme ridiculousness of the whole situation. Really these two, sitting up there like imitation gangsters! He did the worst thing possible and giggled.

There was no waiting for the crash of broken glass this time. The fair boy was out and standing beside Martin in a second, and Lennie seemed about to charge forward out of his chair. Remembering the part he was supposed to be playing, however, he sank heavily back into it again.

"There's a few things you'd better remember," he said, "when you come into my room."

Martin cocked one eyebrow and put his head on one side.

"And you can take that expression off your face! One, nobody comes in here without knocking. Two, my name isn't Lennie nor Leonard to you; it's No. 1. Three, the next time you come you wait for me to speak first!"

"I haven't actually spoken," said Martin mildly, still obeying his inner prompter, "and I don't really expect I shall come again. I'm rather busy."

The fair boy gave him a sharp kick on the ankle, and No. 1 looked more than ever like an angry bull.

"That's for me to decide," he said. "What I say goes here. Perhaps you'd like to know why?"

Martin nodded, as nonchalantly as he could. The kick had landed on the tenderest tip of his ankle bone and hurt; his eyes were watering and he did not trust himself to speak.

"Because I can make them, see?" No. 1 leaned forward again. "Because if they don't do what I want there's accidents can happen. Nothing that I'm going to put a name to, but you'll find it's things that the housing chaps don't like at all, they'll charge it up to your people on the bill. And if they think you're going on doing it, they'll move you away in the end; we got one lot of people we didn't like out that way the other day. And of course with you there's another thing. Show him, Trev."

So floppy-hair was Trev. Before Martin could realise what was happening Trev had shot out a hand and tweaked off his glasses. He snatched out for them but the fair boy caught his wrist and gave it a savage twist. From out of the resulting blurr his voice sounded more jarring than ever, like a fog-horn on the river.

"See? Chaps with glasses has to be specially polite and careful. Specs cost money now."

Trevor hung them mockingly on Martin's finger, and he put them back in their place. He was having extreme difficulty in holding on to his temper; he wanted to stop himself lashing out in all directions to do as much harm as he could to these two before they inevitably got him down and smashed his glasses. After a minute or two he succeeded in getting himself calmer.

"Is that all?" he said. He didn't see that any of this had got anyone much further.

"No it isn't, and it isn't for you to ask either!" Forgetting his role of gangster smoothness, Lennie's voice was now almost shrill with rage. His hair seemed to stand straight up in his fury and he pushed it down again roughly.

"What I brought you here to tell you is this," he said, controlling himself with difficulty: "We're organised in this row, and it's run the way I like it. There's things that I want doing, and it's you and the other chaps that get them done for me. I like my shoes clean and I like my suits brushed. There's things I like to eat and papers I like to look at, and I haven't always got the time or the convenience to go and get them. That's where you come in. I haven't thought what your job's going to be yet, nor whether it will always be the same, but you'll know soon enough and when you know you'd better do it double-quick or else. If you play along of us you'll find we're a nice happy family. If you don't——"

He looked at Trev, and Trev made a gesture as of spitting on his hands and rubbing them together. "You haven't started well, no, not by a long chalk you haven't. You watch your step. Now you can hop it." And he nodded once more to Trevor, who opened the door with one hand and gave Martin a sudden push through it with the other. In the passage he cannoned into Lennie's mother.

"Did you bring his breakfast things, dear?" she asked anxiously.

"No," said Martin shortly, "I didn't. He says he'll do them himself." And he went out into the street.

CHAPTER

5

AT No. 7 Martin found his mother resting in a swept and garnished living-room, with the milk for their elevenses warming on the stove. For almost the first time since she had been there, Mrs. Singer was looking out of the window.

"It's a place that's been let go something dreadful," she said doubtfully; "I don't know how we'll ever manage to smarten it up. I'm sure I don't know what your Aunt Emmeline will say." She looked out once again at the waste of mud and broken bottles and Martin knew that she was comparing it with the trim, square garden and the faultlessly clipped hedge of Emandalf.

"Seems to me that even if we were to put a tub of flowers out, someone would come and break them off. Just look at those kids! Don't seem to have any other thought but to destroy things!" And from his corner of the window, Martin could see the figure of Rusty, bored and listless, going along and kicking down milk bottles, just as a country child might shuffle through autumn leaves.

He glanced at his mother and her disconsolate face worried him. He knew that, ever since she had first heard about the flat, her great ambition was to be able to show Aunt Emmeline a place that was twice as polished and shining as her own, in answer to all the taunts and slights she had endured. It wasn't an ambition that he himself would ever have entertained, but if that was what she wanted, then that was what she should have. He was fond of his mother, and they had been through a lot together at Babbler's Green. In the middle of his own troubles, he registered it as a vow.

"Still—" his mother brightened, as though she had somehow read his thoughts; she turned away from the window and poured frothing cocoa into their mugs—"it's nice inside and it's our own. Emmeline's going up north to Alfred's people for a month or two, and there's no knowing what we mightn't get done to it in that length of time. Mr. Triplett seems a nice old gentleman, and he says that the woman in the top flat's friendly enough too, for all she's a foreigner. Now, shall we get on then?"

Once more, as though they had been two dockers unloading a ship, they started tossing furniture to each other, Martin working like a fury so that he wouldn't have time to feel bothered about No. 1, hoping that behind his violent physical activity his mind might be doing some private thinking for him, in a way it had, and suddenly present him with a way out of his difficulties.

By lunch-time, the middle room was done and they retreated into the sitting-room to eat their picnic hunks of bread and cheese; by tea-time his own room was swept down and washed out, the pattern of vine leaves clearer and more delicate across the ceiling, the indignant spiders shaken out on the end of a broom into the garden. Martin pinned up his two favourite posters on the wall, the small snapshot of Rufus and the photo of his father in his war uniform, and then went out to where his mother had at last managed to get her bowl of water to the long window in the passage.

It was a fascinating process to watch; as she rubbed one patch of window clear, a corresponding patch of sunlight shone through onto the swept stone passage, each one growing larger and larger until at last, like bits of mercury running together, they all ran into one great pool of sunshine, a duplicate window reflected on the floor. Its top reached exactly to the bottom of the staircase, and as he walked round it, imagining himself to be a fly walking round the real window, Martin suddenly found himself beneath the well of the stairs and heard a sudden shuffle above him as though someone had quickly moved. He finished his fly's journey quickly and sighed. So they were at it again.

His mother was looking out of the window she had cleaned, and from behind Mr. Triplett's closed door the whirr of the sewing-machine went on like a captive bee.

"Might do something with that, one of these days," she said vaguely, looking down the stony strip of garden. "Mr. Triplett says it belongs just to the two of us, but he's not interested." Then she turned away. It was evident that her real target was the front of the house, for no matter how unexpected or beautiful the back might become, it was the front by which Aunt Emmeline would enter and judge it.

Her eyes took on a faraway look as her thoughts went back to the matter uppermost in her mind. That red paint on the front door could be washed and perhaps even repainted, if they had enough money left; the brass lion's-head knocker would polish up beautifully. It was old, that, and had class. They would clean up the windows—which made all the difference in the world to a place—put window boxes with a little bit of all sorts in them for some colour. But what about above and in front? The thought of the dreary façade and the wasted mudpatch in front of it temporarily defeated her. Unconsciously using the same methods as Martin, she snatched up the nearest broom and swept vigorously down the passage once more, as though she would show any dust that dared to settle who was the master here. As she reached the front door in a great rush of energy, it was suddenly opened inwards and she fell in a cloud of dust motes into the arms of Mr. Singer, who was coming in with a large bunch of flowers.

"Cor!" Words failed him as he looked at the shining duplicate window in front of him on the floor and its original at the end of the passage, at the handrail of the staircase which Mrs. Singer had polished for as far up as she deemed it to be her territory, at the glimpses of immaculate rooms behind the three open doors. They also failed Mrs. Singer as she sniffed at the bunch of early chrysanthemums and orange dahlias, filled out with spikes of goldenrod and rosy phlox.

"They'll look a treat in the big copper jug," she said. "I've given it a shine. Kettle's on. I'll put them up to their necks in water and do them properly after tea."

"After we've done our shopping, love," Mr. Singer reminded her. "Shops close at six. Have you got the list?" She took it out and they sat happily over the table with it, large cups of tea in front of them which they stirred idly as they looked at the piece of paper, adding things here and putting a cross beside them there as they decided what was to be bought and in what order of importance.

"Lampshades at Woolworth's and a chest of drawers for young Martin at the second-hand shop," concluded his father. "Thought I saw one that'd just do as I came past it just now. You ready, son?"

Martin nodded and they set off, the two grown-ups so absorbed in their own plans and discussions that they scarcely noticed the listless groups of children, or the curiosity with which they and Martin were watched. They walked straight across to the opening that led out on to the outer pavement, and turned down past the privet hedge towards the shops.

From the outer world Martin looked back at Songberd's Grove and became increasingly fidgety, walking slower and slower.

"Step up, son!" He looked at his father and suddenly stopped.

"Do you mind if I don't come? You get any sort of

chest for me, Dad—I'm sure it will be all right." He looked anxiously back towards No. 7, frightened that they would make him go with them after all.

Mr. and Mrs. Singer looked at each other.

"Well, not if he doesn't want to, love," said Mrs. Singer; to shop without Martin, who tended to follow up strange trails in shops, like a dog after rabbits, was much easier. "Here's the keys, then." And, handing them over to Martin, she and her husband went on. For a second Martin watched their familiar and comfortable figures down the road and then he turned back. He was worried about whoever it was that shuffled about at the top of the staircase; he felt almost certain now that there must be two gangs at work.

CHAPTER

6

HOW FOOLISH he had been ever to think of leaving the flat empty! Until he had found out a few more things about the other inhabitants of the house, it was a very unwise thing to do. It was lucky, he thought, that it was holiday-time, without school to add further complications. He swiftly walked back to the door of No. 7.

Inside all was quiet, too quiet, as though his coming had laid an instant stillness on the flat. There was no whirring from Mr. Triplett's sewing-machine and not even any active smell of cooking from upstairs. The sun, which in the morning had come in through the extreme left-hand, eastern edge of his window, had now travelled the whole way across the house and shone obliquely from the western side of the long window in the hall; its rosy light danced with a million dust motes, as though in mockery of Mrs. Singer's efforts. Feeling as though he were stepping into a bath of pink water, Martin moved forward and stood blinking for a moment in the queer, transformed hall.

The stillness and colour of the light gave an eerie quality to everything; he had an uncomfortable feeling that whenever he moved someone else did too, stopping at exactly the same moment as he did. He jumped and then stood still again to test it, scattering dust. Suddenly from his own room there came a resounding sneeze.

He was inside in a moment and ran to the French window. The person in his room was a girl, and as she struggled first with the catch, trying to get out, and then with his hands, a stream of black hair hung down and hid her face. She fought like a cat for a moment, then he got her by both her thin wrists. She winced quickly and suddenly stopped fighting; threw back her head so that her hair fled back with it and stood staring at Martin with the largest, blackest eyes that he had ever seen.

"Let go of my wrist," she said, "it hurts."

Martin loosened his grip a little and looked down at her wrists. On one of them, spreading out from the bone, was a large blue bruise. So she had been the intruder of last night, too. He let go of it and then rolled up his own sleeve to let her see the mark on his forearm, two semicircles of red dents, where he had been bitten last night.

The girl looked back at him for a moment, so intensely that she seemed to be pouring her black gaze over him like a liquid, then suddenly and flashingly she smiled, showing the pointed white teeth that had left their mark.

"I am sorry," she said with curious formality; "it was unavoidable."

"Well, I'm sorry about the other, too," said Martin doubtfully, "but what were you doing here? Why—?"

"Should we sit down?" she said lightly. Her chin was in the air and she seemed in complete control of the situation. "Then I could explain." The actual words that she spoke were in perfect English, but from time to time, she used them in an odd way that made them sound foreign.

Rather grudgingly Martin pushed the chair from his table towards her and sat down on the edge of his bed. He was put out. He had caught this girl red-handed in his room and proved that she was the marauder of last night; right, justice and everything else were on his side, and yet somehow, by the extreme loftiness of her manner, she was managing to make it seem the other way round. Somewhere at the back of his mind he had a suspicion that she was beating him at his own game.

He fished down into the bed, and brought out the shawl. "Is this what you came for?" he said disdainfully, and held it out to her rather as Trevor had held out his glasses to him.

She nodded, took it with a sweeping gesture and let it flutter down into a heap on her lap. "It is my mother's," she said, and then suddenly her eyes flashed as though someone were about to contradict her. "My mother is a very great dancer—La Golondrina, the swallow—that's Spanish, you know."

Unimpressed, Martin merely turned the blank circles of his glasses towards her.

"And last night," he said, with heavy sarcasm, "she was dancing in our garden, I suppose."

The girl turned to him in a fury. "No, I came down for some herbs we planted there! But she might have been!" And at the thought of it her enormous eyes suddenly seemed to blaze and stretch wider across her narrow face. "If she should ever decide to dance there and you should see her by moonlight, as she used to dance in Spain . . . !" She looked at him as though he would then have been blessed by a sight passing mortal belief. She half rose out of the chair as if to demonstrate, then, shaking her head, sank back again and looked at him despondently. "I can't dance, you know," she said. "I haven't inherited it."

Martin was getting exasperated. What did he care whether she danced or didn't dance, whether her whole family danced or not, for that matter? He was beginning to think of them as a series of whirling dervishes and it was making him feel giddy. Who was this mad creature who seemed to have fluttered into his room like a moth, anyway? Was there no end to the extraordinary people that London could produce?

"My mother and father will be back soon," he said sternly. "I think you'd better start explaining."

"Oh, I told you!" She looked surprised. "I came down for herbs. We live in the top flat and we planted them there in the garden; your flat has been empty for so long. I put on trousers—they're easier for the ladder." She looked at him and smiled ingratiatingly. "I have been wondering, too, so much what you would look like. I have tried to see down from upstairs."

To come and peer at him by moonlight, at midnight, thought Martin, seemed rather exaggerated curiosity. He was about to say so when she darted a quick, inquisitive look. "What is your name?"

"Martin Singer."

"Martin. Oh. Martin is nice; like St. Martin who gave his cloak to the beggar. My name is Geneva," she said proudly. "It is where I was born. My mother was—is," she contradicted herself, "so famous that she has danced all over Europe."

She stared at him to let this information sink in, and then started fidgeting with the fringe of the shawl, looking up and down at him beneath her lashes as though trying to make up her mind to ask him a question. Suddenly she seemed to decide. "Are you one of them?" she asked quickly.

"One of them?"

"No. 1," she said haughtily and briefly, "and all that nonsense!" But as though to belie her last words she half-rose from her chair, ready to fly if he said he was. "I saw you go along there this morning."

Martin looked at her and felt a relief so great that it was as though someone had opened a window on a stifling day and let in a flood of fresh air. So at least there was someone, however peculiar, who wasn't in this general conspiracy!

He shook his head. "Of course not."

The atmosphere between them eased perceptibly and Geneva sat down again.

"It's nice here," she said, throwing back her head so that her face was in the glow of the slanting sunlight looking up at the ceiling and walls of Martin's room. "We've got the top floor, you know, that used to be bedrooms. They're quite pretty, but not as splendid as this." She sighed, and then, getting up quickly, took a few steps forward with outstretched hand, and with a faraway look in her eyes and a little formal smile, dropped a slow, sedate curtsy. "One feels what rooms are used to," she explained.

"I like your pictures." Suddenly rising from her curtsy in a kind of twirl she was standing by the wall and looking at one of his posters, tracing with her finger the shape of the letters beneath it.

"They do it all, you know." Her thoughts changing as quickly as her movements, she was standing with her back to the poster again and looking down at Martin.

"Do what?"

"What they say they will; break milk bottles, mess things up, crack your windows, puncture tyres. Luckily we are on the top floor, and I fetch our milk from the shop now. I don't think No. 1 usually bothers much with girls anyway, but he thought when we first came that I would be useful to do some sewing for him, embroider a monogram on his precious dressing-gown. Me! For him!" Her narrow face grew almost old with anger for a moment. "Well, I didn't. And I don't know what he thought about it because I haven't been out the front way since." She shrugged her shoulders.

"Then how do you get out?"

She looked at him, anxiously. "You saw. Last night. But it's your garden now."

"It's all right with me," said Martin, bestowing the freedom of the garden upon her with a sweeping gesture, "and I'm sure my parents won't mind." But he spoke a little absent-mindedly, his thoughts being occupied with larger issues. To make someone use the back entrance of her own house! It was a completely intolerable state of affairs and one which he would rapidly have to alter.

"How many of them are there?" he asked, and, unexpected though all her actions were, he was totally unprepared for Geneva's reaction to this simple question.

With eyes ablaze she slid down from the window-sill where she had gone to perch, ran to take hold of both his arms above the elbow and gazed into his face with such excitement that, just as he had been by the long, sunset window, he seemed to be bathed once again in some unreal and unearthly light.

"You mean we're going to fight them!" she cried, and at the use of the plural pronoun, Martin looked back at her in surprise.

It had not occurred to him that he would be anything but alone in this venture, and she put his thoughts in such a whirl that he was far from sure whether she would be more of a help or a hindrance.

But to have somebody with him, and particularly someone in the same house. . . . He suddenly remembered last night. She hadn't then seemed to be lacking in either energy or determination.

He looked at her doubtfully, then nodded. "Of course," he said.

A key grated in the distant front door and the handle started to turn.

"Oh, come upstairs to our flat to talk about it!" cried Geneva. "My mother won't be back yet." And they ran hastily out onto the balcony, where Martin followed her up the fire-escape and into the most astonishing room that he had ever yet seen.

CHAPTER

7

GENEVA'S MOTHER had indeed been a dancer, the child also of two dancers who wandered about Spain. She had been born in a cave outside Granada which at that time served them for a home, and almost the first thing of which she had been conscious was the darting and swooping flight of the swallows across the mouth of the cave. Perhaps the patterns that they wove through the air then entered deep into her spirit, for when she grew up to dance her way out of the villages into the towns and out of the towns into nation-wide fame she was nicknamed after the birds she had so often watched.

At the height of her success, when she was dancing

through Europe, she had met an Englishman, loved and married him. He was gay and charming but no one had known that he was really very ill; when he died, La Golondrina stopped dancing. The small, black-eyed Geneva was then two years old, and there was a firm idea in her mother's mind that a house in England would be a better background for her daughter than another cave.

The Englishman had given her the address of his parents, and she imagined they were rich, but as he only wrote to them when the fancy took him, and never stayed long enough in the same place to get an answer, the address, since he had last known it, had changed. After a long and terrible journey, La Golondrina found herself in London one day, standing with Geneva in the street outside a house where total strangers now lived, who were unable to help her. It was raining and she could speak no English; despair settled round her like a black shawl. But still she clung to the idea that England was where Geneva must be brought up.

She had come with some money tied round her waist, and somehow, no one will ever know how, had managed to find a room. When the money seemed to be nearing its end, she pulled herself together and went round the theatres to try and dance again, but nobody had heard of her in England and she only succeeded in being taken on at one of them as a sort of extra dresser and general help. She earned just enough money to keep herself and Geneva.

She had left the first room she found and moved on from one to another. Finally, flinging down her fans and her shawls and her one precious book of press cuttings, she came to rest in the top rooms of No. 7, and had stayed in Songberd's Grove ever since.

But not forever! Oh no. There were only a few ideas in La Golondrina's head but they were firm ones. Geneva must be educated in England, true; but was not she, La Golondrina, a dancer? When the education was finished, she would go back to Spain. Here, in England, they did not understand dancing. Every night when she got back from the theatre she would talk about it to her daughter, remembering the rosy past and describing an even more glorious future which awaited them, full of roses and sunshine and music and fame. Wide-eyed, Geneva listened, long after the time when she ought to have been asleep; accepting completely the legend of her mother, La Golondrina, the beautiful and swallow-like dancer. What neither of them stopped to consider, and indeed could hardly even see, so carried away were they by their hopes and enthusiasm, was that La Golondrina had become far from swallow-like now. For, alas, she had become extremely fat.

La Golondrina

Sometimes, particularly when it was cold or rained, her thoughts became too much for her and the prospect of returning to Spain too far off, and whenever this happened the black shawl of despair fell about her again. She knew only one consolation, to cook and to eat; and like snow piling up round a snowman, the flesh slowly piled up round La Golondrina. Among the earliest memories of her childhood, merging with the sound of the guitars and laughter and singing, and the evening flight of the swallows, was the smell of the wonderful dishes that had come from the back of the cave as her mother cooked. Now, as she created once again the same dishes and smells for Geneva and herself, she seemed to be able to make Spain and hope come flowing into the dingy little London rooms, and the waiting did not seem to be so long.

In Songberd's Grove she had really let herself go. The sight that met Martin's eye as he stepped off the top of the fire-escape might have come straight from *The Arabian Nights*, and the smell made him blink and sneeze.

Onions hung everywhere, in great bunches of pinky-brown globes; from the door-handles and the catches of the windows were festooned pearly-white and red strings of garlic and red peppers. Large peppers, parrot-green and scarlet, lay about on cupboard tops and window-sills, among sprigs of withering herbs and bowls of olives, the artificial flowers that La Golondrina made for the theatre and the brilliant scraps of her own departed glory. Strings of dried fungi, of various sinister shapes and colours, were hung wherever an accommodating knob could be found to hold them, and from inside the bursting cupboard doors inordinate quantities of rice, cheese and spaghetti, as though they had to feed a houseful for many months, were visible. There was a basin of empty mussel shells and a straw-covered bottle of olive oil in front of the empty fireplace and a saucepan was bubbling and brewing strange odours from the side of the stove. All round, through and above everything floated a smell of hot oil and spices.

Looking at something which, although he could hardly believe it, seemed to be a puff-ball, thinking confusedly of Aunt Emmeline's string shopping-bag and kitchen cupboard, and of the carrots, sprouts and boiling-fish to which she was most addicted, Martin stood staring until Geneva pulled him over to a shawl-covered couch in the corner.

"This was worn by my mother, La Golondrina, in Seville!" she said with pride. "Look, this was her fan, and here is her photograph." But before Martin could really take in the faded brown picture of a slim figure fluttering in shawls and flounces, Geneva was off again.

"Tell me," she said. "Quickly! What are we going to do?"

Martin took off his glasses and wiped off the thin steaming film which seemed to be settling on them, then he looked down at the faded, once splendid crimson shawl on which he sat and felt the embroidered flowers with his fingers. It was very different from Aunt Emmeline's plush.

"Your eyes are a beautiful colour—do you always wear those things?" said Geneva suddenly and inconsequently, and to Martin's embarrassment and disgust, he felt that he was blushing.

He put the glasses on again and looked at her sternly. Fully dressed, as he now considered himself to be, he was more in control of the situation, but he felt he could have thought much more clearly in less exuberant surroundings. He wanted to get all the facts clear, point by point.

"How many of them did you say there were?" he asked again.

From the floor opposite him, where she had flung herself down on a shabby bit of fur that did duty for a rug, Geneva held up one hand and counted on her fingers.

"There's No. 1," she said, "Leonard Byre, dear Len, or Lennie." And she made a face that was eloquent of all she felt. "There's Trevor, the tall boy with the yellow hair, and then the one that looks dirty all over—I don't know his name."

"Mudface," said Martin.

Geneva nodded. "Mudface will do. He usually brings the messages. Then there's the Irish one. I don't really think he likes it—I think he might almost come over to us if we had any way of getting hold of him. And then of course there are all the little ones. They're clever with those; they make them do all the breaking and kicking and paint-picking for them, make it into a sort of game. Then they say that they don't know who did it, and that it's nobody's fault. There was a lilac tree outside when we first came here," she added, inconsequently again.

Martin looked up in question.

"They stripped it. Every leaf, every shoot: They even got the bark off in the end. It was the same with Mr. Bolsom's yellow door."

Once more Martin looked up.

"At No. 6, the next house to us," Geneva pointed. "The Bolsoms are an old couple—perhaps you've seen them?—and he used to be a painter; I think he still does a few odd jobs here and there. Well, he got permission from the Housing Officer to paint the front door; we are all allowed to do our own if we want.

Oh, it was the most lovely yellow!" She clasped her hands in front of her for a moment as she remembered it.

"He burnt all the old paint off with one of those blow-lamp things, then he painted it; first a sort of pinkish under-colour and then that yellow—oh, it was like canaries and mimosa and all the yellow things you can ever think of. It made it look as though the sun was shining, even though it was raining. They slept with it open, the last night, in case it stuck."

"Well?" said Martin impatiently.

Geneva looked at him. "Nobody could say who'd done it, whether it was an accident or what, but in the morning it had somehow got all burnt off again, melted and smeared, with some of it scorched and lots of the pink showing underneath. Mr. Bolsom just left it—he didn't seem to have the heart to do any more. He never has since either. It made a difference to him—he looks older."

As Martin remembered the door, now striped like a rotten banana, next door to them, anger and a sudden fear came into his heart. It was worse than he thought. Why did they do it? What was the point of it all? But could the thing that had happened to Mr. Bolsom happen to his mother? Could she give up and grow suddenly older too? Something must be done about it, and at once.

"Which of the houses do they live in?" he asked.

"They're all up at the other end," answered Geneva, "Lennie in No. 1, of course, and Trevor next door in No. 2. There's nobody important in No. 3, and Mudface and the one you call Rusty are in No. 4."

"It wouldn't be very easy to get hold of Rusty then," Martin considered the possibilities. "But it leaves two clear houses between us and them. Who lives in those?"

"All grown-ups in No. 6. The Bolsoms are on the ground floor, and two lots of women, who go out cleaning, in the two flats up above. They're all friends, and they squawk at the children sometimes and shoo at them like hens, but nobody pays any attention to them. In No. 5 there are only small ones. Three Irish families they are and the mothers do nothing but talk and quarrel. But it really is very lucky that they are all down at the other end because it makes the garden safe." She got up to point through the open window and down on to the strip of stones and rubble below.

Martin joined her, to take stock of their position and see how wide a field of vision could be had from each window. Could they be overlooked by Mudface in No. 4? But from one window you could only see as far as two gardens away, so they were safe. As though the gardens had at sometime been more than mere cat runs, the tops of the walls between them were decorated with small but effective spikes, so that a raid along the wall tops was impossible too. As long as he and Geneva kept the front door shut they were impregnable; it was something, if not much.

"What about the door at the end of the garden?" Martin had just caught sight of it, leading out into the side street.

Geneva gave him a sidelong glance, slid a hand into her cotton dress that looked too skimpy to hide anything and produced a large key on the end of a string. She looked at it as it lay on the palm of her hand and then took it off her neck to hand it reluctantly towards Martin.

"You keep it," he said off-handedly. "As long as I know where it is." And her eyes brightened as she quickly put it away again. Its possession evidently meant a lot to her and he had not the heart to tell her that, for himself, he would consider it a most mistaken and ignominious thing ever to go out by that back door. Then another thought occurred to him.

His own motives in this thing were quite clear, but what were Geneva's? It was better to know.

"Why do you want to do all this," he asked, "if you're quite happy to go out through the garden and they don't bother you any more?"

Geneva's eyes snapped. "Because I hate them!"

she said briefly and sufficiently. "And for when my mother dances again," she added as an afterthought. Unlike her mother, she always imagined a triumph in England too.

Martin looked at her, puzzled.

"It is not a very good place for reporters and photographers to come to, is it?" she said, with a withering gesture. She had worked out the picture of the return of La Golondrina to the last detail.

Well, that being settled, what were they going to do?

For a moment or two they stood silent and thinking, staring down at the garden and watching the dusk that was beginning to fill its corners and steal some of the colours from the gaudy room behind them.

"Two of us and four of them," said Geneva pensively, leaning on the balcony rail with her chin in her hands, "and Leonard and Trevor are both older and bigger—but of course not so clever as you!" She turned on him in a flash as though she might have offended him, but all she did was to interrupt the train of his thoughts.

If only she would keep quiet for a moment! It was like having a squib for a confederate. What had he been thinking? Oh yes.

"Has everyone taken sides?" he asked. "Have we counted absolutely everyone?"

She thought, counted on her fingers again, and nodded her head, then suddenly, her hair flying back again, shot up like a jack-in-the-box.

"Everyone so far!" she said. "But there are the new ones coming down below, of course. We must get them. Three of them there are, I saw it on the Housing Officer's list. Well, they're not likely to be three grown-ups, two parents and a child most likely, or a widow, perhaps, and two," she added hopefully. "Oh, wouldn't it be lovely if they were two enormous boys!"

"Just as likely two infant girls," said Martin, but nevertheless, faint though it was, there did seem to be a glimmering of hope there.

"How shall we get them?" Once again, with her bubbling, Geneva was making it difficult for him to think.

He waved her aside as though she had been a fly. "Be nice to them, of course. How did we feel when we first arrived? You want friendliness, not threats. We——"

"We'll ask them to tea!" cried Geneva. "Write them an invitation in a letter and make sure that they get it the very first thing. We could have it up here—my mother is away all day. She would make pastries, turron—oh, lovely things for us! How lucky that we are all in the same house!"

Tea had not exactly been Martin's idea, but he saw that it would do. He nodded. "You do the inside part then, and I'll wait outside and see that nobody speaks to them before we do. Which day do they come?"

"Thursday. Oh, Martin, you will be careful. There are so many of them and only one of you!" A ridiculous remark, but oddly enough, Martin felt rather pleased. Extraordinary and tiresome creature though she might be, there was something a little warming and flattering in her concern. He was beginning to smile at her reassuringly when——

"Martin!" His mother's voice echoed up the stairs and he shot to his feet.

"We can use the front way now," said Geneva, and she let him out at the top of the staircase. "Oh, there's my mother coming up too!" She stood watching his descending red head, and for the dark one to appear.

As Martin saw the immensely stout woman with melancholy dark eyes who was labouring up the stairs, he whistled soundlessly and shook his head. It seemed to him that it would be a long time before Geneva got her photographers, her reporters, before La Golondrina would be dancing again.

CHAPTER

8

GETTING BACK to his own flat, after the highly spiced brilliance of Geneva's, was rather like stepping ashore on English soil again after a visit to some parrot-haunted tropical island. Martin drew several deep breaths and felt his head clearing with each one.

The sitting-room was temporarily upside down again with his parents' new purchases.

"Give me a hand with this, son," said his father, as he went in, and when they got back from depositing the new and satisfactory chest of drawers in Martin's room, they put up the mirror together over the mantelpiece. By the window his mother was fussing anxiously over six little green plants in pots.

"Polyanthus," she explained, leaving them none the wiser. "A terrible extravagance, but the flower shop was selling them cheap. Still, it's money well spent: plant them in the autumn and you get twice as fine a show in the spring. And if—I don't really expect she will, mind you—but if Emmeline were to come earlier, it would be something . . . I thought we could just put the pots out on the window-sill, they would look pretty there, till your father could knock up a window-box."

"Not in the front?" cried Martin quickly.

"Well, of course, love, where else?" And as Mrs. Singer threw up the window sash to put them out, Martin shook his head.

If only she would wait to do things until he told her. If only she could realise how carefully one had to go! In the moment before she drew the window down again he thought he caught a glimpse of Mudface's watching eyes. He remembered the lilac tree and Mr. Bolsom and felt worried.

Then he suddenly thought of something else. "I should bring your bike in, if I were you, Dad," he said. "There's an awful lot of broken glass about and you never know what those kids will get up to."

His father looked at him for a moment and then nodded his head. "Maybe you're right."

"There's Mr. Triplett coming in tonight, don't forget."

Martin looked at the clock. "How long before supper?" he asked.

"Well, say in about half an hour."

It was still fairly light. As Martin went back to his own room, he paused uncertainly for a moment, looking at his things; then he wandered out onto the balcony and down the three steps into the garden.

It was no good trying to concentrate on anything now; so much had happened to him in the last twenty-four hours, and it was all so bewildering, that he felt he must go somewhere where he could quietly get it sorted out. He hoped to goodness that Geneva wouldn't see him out of her window and call down to him, but mercifully all was quiet. Walking up and down the garden like a captain on his quarter-deck, his hands in his pockets and his eyes on the ground, he tried to think.

What *was* he going to do? Nothing like this had ever happened to him before. He had only arrived here yesterday, looking forward to nothing more than a quiet time in his own place and peace to get on with his own things, and now, before he knew where he was, and partnered only by an extraordinary Spanish girl, he seemed to have taken on the whole street. Not that there was any alternative; he was peaceable by nature but he wasn't going to allow himself to be messed about by anyone like Lennie and his crew.

Lennie! At the thought of his ridiculous, clown-like figure and gangster set-up, Martin snorted. What was wrong with people like Lennie, what fun did they get out of all that nonsense, and of doing nothing but destroying things? He thought again of the outside of Songberd's Grove and what they had turned it into and his gloom deepened.

He wasn't going to stand by and watch his mother going the way Mr. Bolsom had—of that he was determined. Come to that, merely as a matter of Singer pride, he wasn't so keen himself that his aunt should see the place as it was now. But what could he do? As he reached the end of the garden and turned again, he frowned in a desperate attempt to reach some solution.

Paint their door? Even if that were red again, the window-boxes installed and burgeoning with greenery, the brass lion's-head knocker shining, Aunt Emmeline would still have to approach it across the mud flats strewn with glass; would gaze, while she waited for the bell to be answered, at the disastrous, streaky paint next door. Aunt Emmeline was very keen on what she called the tone of the neighbours. Martin snorted again. It would do her a power of good to live here for a month or two; then she would come across some pretty queer tones! But he brought his mind back to the matter in hand. To impress Aunt Emmeline was what his mother wanted; as long as he could do anything about it, that was what she would have.

Could heart be put back into the Bolsoms to repaint their own door? Could he and Geneva perhaps do it for them? If they did, was there any way of patrolling the two houses so that the paint stayed put? Night and day it would have to be, and only two of them to do it. He shook his head despondently and turned once again, so that he was facing the house. There was a possibility of more help from there, but not very much and he couldn't reckon on it: whoever it was who came might even turn out to be another Lennie; then, with enemies in the house, as well as without, they really would be sunk.

What to do? The question seemed to meet him at each turn of his walk. If only there were someone whose advice he could ask!

Oddly enough it never occurred to him to bring his parents into this; it was something that had to be settled, as it had started, below the grown-up level. He thought longingly of Mr. Acle, who had always seemed to him to be someone entirely on his own, belonging to neither class.

Not only had he learnt how to cut letters, and the

forms of various alphabets, from Mr. Acle, but also a certain amount of practical philosophy. Living alone among his blocks of stone, the old mason had evolved a working theory of life for himself, which he was always ready to pass on to Martin. How he wished he had him here! Martin kicked at a stone in the failing light and wondered what he would say.

"Whenever you get to the point when you don't seem able to do anything—" so quickly and so suitably that it nearly made him jump, the memory of that gruff and placid voice came back to Martin—"do what's nearest to hand. There's always something that you've overlooked and while you're doing that the further-off things have got a way of arranging themselves out . . ."

He could even remember the time and the place when Mr. Acle had said that, standing by his latest memorial and looking it critically up and down.

"Many's the time I've been scratching me head for the shape of a face or a wing, when there was some polishing or chipping I could have been doing, and while I got down to it the other things took care of themselves."

Well, that was all very well, but what was nearest to hand here? He kicked at the stone again, picked it up and was surprised to find how smooth it was. Of course, there was always this garden. It wasn't much to begin on but still it would be something; he could start by tidying it up: heap all the stones to one side and plant some green stuff down the middle. Then if Aunt Emmeline came on a fine day, perhaps she could be whisked unnoticing through the front door and straight out into the garden. Greatly relieved to have some definite and practical thing to do, Martin looked round to consider where to begin and then bent to pick up some stones. He could have a rockery, for rockeries were among the things which his aunt considered to have very high tone.

It was almost twilight now, and the pale surfaces of the houses all round him gleamed dimly, like enormous cliffs. There was a heavy and rather ominous feeling in the air, as though it might thunder. As Martin went to and fro with his stones, bending and straightening and carrying automatically, his thoughts wandered back to Lennie. He wondered when he would get his first message and what stupid thing he would be asked to do. He couldn't have made himself very popular this morning. At the thought of his inner prompter, and of the trouble into which it always led him, he sighed.

Did everyone have one? He would never know—it was not a thing you could ever ask. As he went on moving the stones, humping ever larger and larger ones now, he amused himself by thinking of it as a person and wondering what its face would be like. He turned over a large stone, got his hands round it and was just going to move it when he dropped it with a cry.

Lying on the dark earth beneath it and staring up at the sky, as though it were in fact the very embodiment of the conscience he had been thinking about, was a face.

Repressing a wild desire to scream, backing a few steps away from it with his hand over his mouth, Martin stared down.

It was alive! But no, how could it be? It must be carved in the stone. He looked at it and the longer he looked the more fascinated with it he became. Eventually he knelt and touched it with a cautious finger tip. Cold and yet oddly responsive, the familiar feeling of marble came back to him. The face stared up at him and now he saw that it was laughing.

It was so dark now that Martin could hardly discern the features, but even from the pattern of hollows and shadows came the most extraordinary and comforting impression of personality, strength and good humour. Who in the world could it have been? That it was the likeness of an actual, once-living man Martin had no doubt at all. The strange thing was that it reminded him of somebody, someone that he had recently seen.

THE FACE

"Martin!"

And always, at a moment like this, they had to call you in!

Well, he wouldn't have been able to look at it properly until daylight anyway. Hastily scooping up some loose earth and grass, he heaped them over his new find for safety, got up from his knees and ran into the house. As he flicked on his light and paused by the chest of drawers for a moment to give a flying dab at his hair, an even more extraordinary thought came to him. It was his room that it had reminded him of; the expression on the face was like the personality of his room.

"Batty!" he said to himself again and stared at his startled face in the mirror with an expression that was near to panic. He was still shaking his head to get rid of these ridiculous thoughts, like a dog shaking to get the water out of his ear, when he walked into the sitting-room. Mr. Triplett had arrived early and was already there.

CHAPTER

9

THERE ARE three proper steps in taking possession of a place, and Mrs. Singer had gone through all of these correctly. The first, which she had taken yesterday, is to put something of your own in it; the second, be it spring, summer, autumn or winter, is to light your own fire there. The last, and perhaps the most important, is to invite a guest, to seal everything and agree with you that it is indeed your home. Well polished and at ease again, like released prisoners rejoicing in liberty after their long sentence in store, the bits of Singer furniture, with all their friendly dents and scratches, relaxed round the room. The fire purred gently in the grate, and in front of it, sitting in the most comfortably bulging chair and praising everything most satisfactorily, was Mr. Triplett.

He was evidently in the full flow of telling Mr. and Mrs. Singer his life story, warmed up to talking point again and sipping a large cup of tea so hot that it misted the moons of his half spectacles.

Martin slipped into his chair, and, taking the plate that his mother handed over to him, tried to stop thinking of the face in the garden and to listen to the tailor.

"Aye, forty years with Cantrell's I was," the old tailor was saying, shaking his not very stable head. "Started there as apprentice; learnt it all. Trouser cutting, weskit cutting, coat cutting and stitching—and that's where I stayed." An even more remote and dreamy look than usual came into his eyes, as though he were reliving past triumphs.

" 'Never had a man to stitch a coat like you, Tom Triplett,' says Mr. Cantrell. 'There's Captain Owen asking for you and Mr. Lester, and now here's Lord Simon Vigo saying he won't have his coat done by anybody else.' "

He sighed once again and went on, his head shaking like a china mandarin. Lord Simon, superb and dashing, had evidently become his great hero, and now in his old age, all alone in his little room and living in the past, he could think of nobody else. Like an artist remembering all his most successful work, Mr. Triplett recalled all the coats he had made for Lord Simon.

". . . his uniform and all his hunting kit, of course. Then there was that mess jacket and his blue patrols—that was a good job if I ever did one! Every sort of coat you can imagine I made for him—there wasn't anything he didn't do. Hunting, steeplechasing—for all he was so big. Boxing—ah, but that was his real interest! Night after night he'd take a party down to the ring, knew all the names of the boxers and all the young ones who were up and coming. . . ." The old man went on reminiscing, talking as though it were mainly by virtue of the coats made by him, Tom Triplett, that Lord Simon was able to shine at everything he did.

"How could anyone ride properly in a coat that pulled him under the arms, I should like to know?" he demanded fiercely, and then suddenly, with a bump, came back into the present.

"How anyone can do anything in the coats they make nowadays, I don't know," he said gloomily. "All men got to be the same shape, same as they got to think the same way nowadays, I suppose. If I was to see one of my old canvases again it'd be like the man himself sitting opposite me in the chair; tell you in a minute who it was, too, I could. But nowadays . . . not an inch of hand-stitching anywhere, no craft or pride about 'em anywhere." It seemed as if he were going on with his lament forever.

In desperation Mrs. Singer broke in. "Hand-stitching, Mr. Triplett?" she asked, as she filled up his cup, "I never knew coats had to be stitched by hand." And in a welter of information and names and reminiscences all muddled up together, the old man was off again, the name of his hero cropping up over and over again.

Cantrell's had fallen on evil days, it appeared, and had eventually closed down; Mr. Triplett had tried to get another job but was too old; eventually he had got work with some cleaners, doing alterations and repairs for them.

"Well, I suppose I mustn't grumble. It's a safe job and a living wage, but some of the trash they give me to deal with nowadays, Mrs. Singer, you'll hardly believe! Well, that was a very nice cup of tea, that was, and I must be getting along. You've made it very homey, I must say." And looking round the room admiringly, he backed towards the door like a shadow, slipped through it, and was gone.

"Well, just fancy!" said Mrs. Singer. "One lives and learns. I never knew there was all that to tailoring, did you?"

Her husband, fingering his cheap and cheerfully

coloured ready-made suit, shook his head. Martin, his mind temporarily detached from his worries, was basking in the glow from the fire and the warmth of his cocoa, imagining himself in splendid uniform and of splendid proportions, outvying Lord Simon. With the man of his stone face somewhere beside him he was charging the enemy at the head of his men.

"Wonder if women's suits have all that canvas and stitching too?" said Mrs. Singer, whose curiosity was roused, and she went over to feel of her own jacket. "Here's something that feels like it—oh, dear sakes no, it isn't!" With eyes that were round with guilt and apology behind her glasses, she drew something out of the inner pocket and looked at her son apprehensively.

"I really don't know what's coming over me nowadays," she said, "I'll forget to put my shoes on next. Still, I don't expect it's all that important. It's a note for you, love; that tall boy with the nice fair hair asked me to give it to you. Got a club or something down there, have they? Seemed to be a lot of them all together." And she handed him the note.

Arrested in mid-gallop from chasing the enemy, torn away from his peaceful basking, Martin got to his feet and stretched out a hand for it wearily. He glanced at it and the contents were much as he had expected. So Lennie hadn't wasted much time after all.

"No, it's nothing *important*," he said with a fine irony that was lost on his parents, and pecking at their cheeks perfunctorily, as one who had greater things on his mind than mere sentiment, he went off to his room.

Fruit selling off cheap, said the note, in a most unpleasant and ill-informed hand. *Bella Street market. Get some grapefruit before 6. Call here for cash.* And it was signed with a number 2. Trev, he supposed.

Martin sighed. Because of his mother's forgetfulness, the matter had been taken out of his hands. Otherwise he might have thought of some pleasant things to do; his old friend, the inner prompter, was already stirring with suggestions. What a thing to ask him to do! Well, they would have gathered by now that he hadn't, and wasn't, going to get the grapefruit—what would they do? He considered the possibilities, and tried to think at what points he and his parents were vulnerable.

The bicycle was in—thank goodness he had persuaded his father to do that! Tomorrow he would obviously have to get up early enough to be waiting when the milkman came, and take the bottles from his hands. Martin sighed again; getting up early was not one of his favourite exercises. It didn't much matter now if they did pick the paint off the door; according to his plans for the house it was coming off sooner or later anyway. So let them pick away, and off the windows too, if they liked. Window-sills? The plants! That was the most obvious thing for them to do, ruin his mother's precious ten-shillings-worth and strike her the first blow. Well, in that case he must go and get them in. He put his head out through the passage door and listened.

From the sitting-room door now a great deal of noise was coming, the crackling of their wireless as his father adjusted it, the clapping and shouting of the studio audience, and then, as they hushed, the triumphant flaring and blaring of a trumpet. That was all right; his father's one great passion in life was for trumpet music, and, as is the way of music-lovers, the more he enjoyed it, the louder he turned it on, as though to drown himself in the glorious sound. You could drop ten tons of brass in the hall now and he wouldn't hear it till the programme was over; now was the moment to bring in those wretched flowers. Martin opened the front door a crack.

Except for the glimmer of the distant street-lamps all was dark; near to the houses, like a current in the sea, there seemed to be an extra rim of deep, warm black. He tiptoed down the steps and reached to get the first two pots off the sill. It was difficult to get a hold on their round surfaces; they were cold and clammy after Mrs. Singer's watering and smelt of sooty earth, but all the same he managed to get a finger into them and a thumb over their rims and to transfer the first two indoors. Out and in again with the second two, and he was just turning towards the front door with the last ones when a form that had been slinking like a cat along the houses detached itself from the darkness and hurled itself upon him.

It was Rusty, whom he normally could have dealt with easily, but what could he do now? No one had ever got caught in a more ridiculous position. Both of his hands were occupied with pots, so that he couldn't use them; the pots were the whole point of his mission, so he couldn't drop them. Feeling as though they were glued to his hands like giant boxing gloves, trying to use them somehow, but without damaging the plants, he waltzed absurdly round the small figure that was pummelling at him down below. For Rusty, the youngest, smallest and newest of No. 1's lieutenants had been given this job, which they thought would be easy, as his first assignment.

If only there were someone in the hall, thought Martin, desperately, so that he could hand the wretched things inside and deal with Rusty properly! But the trumpet shouted gloriously and happily on and Rusty was cutting off his way in. Using his hips, knees and elbows as though he were dancing some exaggerated Samba, Martin circled wildly round as the Irish boy, full of zeal to perform his first mission properly, tried to snatch at the plants, which were always just out of his reach. While this silly dance was going on, Martin who was trying to edge himself nearer and nearer towards the door, thought he would try the effects of a little propaganda.

"Why don't you leave them, chum?" he whispered breathlessly. "Join up with us and live in peace! We . . ."

In his fury, or the stress of his emotions, Rusty raised his head suddenly to charge again and cracked it on the edge of one of the flower-pots. He let out a howl. From somewhere down the row a door opened and two figures ran out, their feet clattering down the pavement towards him. In the same moment Martin realised something else. The trumpet programme had stopped. As he backed desperately towards the door once more, in a last effort to get there before reinforcements came, he nearly fell over a fleeing cat. Inspiration came to him.

Flinging his head back, he opened his throat and

gave the life-like imitation of a cat's concert which had been his one artistic outlet in the boring garden of Aunt Emmeline. With as much skill as the trumpeter his notes rose and shrilled, so that even the cat stopped for a moment and looked surprised, wondering if it had missed something.

From all round, immediately a dozen windows flew open and a dozen dollops of water flew through the air; this was a common emergency in Songberd's Grove and all were prepared for it. Trev was caught and checked by the Bolsoms' water and Mudface was drenched with some soapy stuff from the women above. Martin and Rusty caught La Golondrina's together, but Martin, who from past experience had been expecting it, ducked quickly, swerved and slid in through the door.

"Cats," he said briefly and unnecessarily to his parents, as they came out into the passage, switched on the light and saw him dripping, with the last two plants. "Heard 'em and thought I'd better bring your treasures in, Ma! They'll be safer on my balcony at the back.

"Think I'll have a bath," he said, hoping by the magnanimity of the offer to stop any further comment, "if that's all right with you?" And in fact the prospect really seemed quite pleasant. Not only was he drenched, but also covered in small bits of earth and leaf that had wobbled off the top of the flower-pots; and La Golondrina's anti-cat water seemed to have the pungent smell of all the rest of her flat.

In the hot and steamy water, staring up at the copper spout of the geyser, he let himself relax.

"Round one to No. 7!" he thought, and as he went back along the passage to his room, in his pyjamas and with his fine, foxy hair sticking up in damp spikes, he swaggered a little, unconsciously, as though he were indeed Lord Simon Vigo returning from battle. The man with the stone face would have been pleased, he thought.

Sleep came to him instantly, for never in his whole life had so many things happened to him in one day. It came before he had time to think about the face again, or indeed about anything at all. In his dreams, while Lord Simon galloped up and down in front of them in a scarlet coat, the newly cleaned and snow-white houses of Songberd's Grove glittered with seven rainbow-coloured doors. As La Golondrina leant out of her window and showered the crowd beneath her with peppers and artificial flowers, Aunt Emmeline, clutching her string shopping-bag, stepped admiringly up to the front door to the accompaniment of a fanfare of cats and trumpets.

But the next morning, as he went sleepily out to intercept the milkman, he saw that the windows all up their house had been punctured with star-splintered, catapulted holes.

CHAPTER

10

A FEW days later, at the other end of the row, No. 1 was standing by the window and thinking. It was not an exercise in which he indulged very often and he found the process troublesome. He kicked his spare pair of shoes across the floor and then picked them up again anxiously to see if he had scratched them; threw up the window and stared out at the empty street, then banged it down again, with its grey curtain flapping, as he paced to the wall and back again.

He was glad that Trev and Alan, which was Mudface's name, weren't about. Silly poops! He was fed up with them. As he stood by the window, the light falling on his dark and frowning features, he groped about in his mind and tried to find out what was worrying him and why he felt as he did.

The main trouble about Lennie was that he had been a beautiful baby; perhaps if he had been a bit less so, squinted or had a blobby nose, things might have turned out differently for him. When strangers had seen the Byre family out together, the two doting parents gazing proudly into the pram, they had been puzzled to tell from where he got his looks. Although his father, who was a boxer by profession, had a superbly muscled body bulging behind his tight suit, and pushed the pram along with a surprising, cat-like grace, his amiable face was so flattened and thickened at all its extremities that it was difficult to tell what it had originally looked like. The features of Lennie's mother had been pretty enough when she was a young girl, but were now as blurred by foolishness as her husband's were by the continual stopping of leathern blows.

Hanging over his pillow and adoring him, thinking that never in the whole history of the world before had there been such perfection, each parent saw entirely different visions of Lennie's future and registered entirely different vows.

His father, who was known as Basher, saw him in the ring, his dark eyes, with their long curling lashes, alert above a pair of darting gloves and dancing feet.

Basher Byre's son! In his mind he promised him the best training and the best equipment, the juiciest steaks, that money earned by his, the Basher's, fists could buy. He saw himself, almost as soon as the baby could walk, running round the park with him and teaching him all that he knew. Happiness glowed in his curranty, puffy-lidded eyes.

At the same moment his mother was vowing quite simply that never, never, never, should her precious and beautiful Lennie go anywhere near a glove or a ring.

Unfortunately for Lennie, Basher went off to the war. Almost as soon as he went into action a bullet hit him above the heart. It felt to his astonished senses like one of the blows delivered by Sooty Abicar, his most constant rival, and he was just stepping mazily and happily forward, to return it with interest, when he dropped down dead. So Lennie was left to fulfill his mother's vow.

The first thing that she did, like a cat carrying its kitten to safety, was to move from where they had been living and leave no address. She was determined that Basher's friends, who were many, and who had known of his plans for Lennie, who had dutifully hung over the pram admiring his length of limb and prodding his infant muscles, should not get a chance to go on with the training that Basher had begun.

After this, her one outburst of craftiness, she lapsed into her original foolishness again, went out to work, and proceeded, like someone unravelling a piece of knitting, quite literally to spoil her son. But somehow and somewhere a few bits of Basher still managed to linger behind.

"What was my dad, Mum?" Lennie was back from his first morning at school. He felt, in some odd way, as though ghostly voices were ringing in his ears, that his father was something to boast about, and then realised to his astonishment that it was a subject that was never mentioned at home, and that he didn't know.

"He was . . . he was a florist, dear," said his mother, searching for the occupation most unlike Basher's real one. "A little, delicate man, ever so artistic; he made lovely wreaths"; and with a sinking feeling in his stomach Lennie went back to school. It was after he had announced this, and heard the snigger that went round the class, that he had first proved, unknown to his mother, that he was Basher's son all right.

He had long been used to getting everything he wanted from his mother; after the damage that he did in this first encounter he managed to get it from his schoolfellows too. It was not long before he came to consider that it was right and proper that he should get everything he wanted, without doing anything for it, from the world. He liked the feeling of power that this gave him and tried it out on everybody he met. The more he could bend them about to his will the more it made him feel that he was somebody (which deep down inside him he secretly doubted), and the dimmer the shadow of the despicable little florist seemed to grow.

He had just established himself nicely at his first school when one day his mother saw one of Basher's old friends at the corner of their street; she came in pale and muttering, pulled up stakes and moved within three days. She went to an entirely different part of London and took the rooms in Songberd's Grove.

At the new school, history repeated itself; it wasn't the profession of Lennie's father that caused mirth this time, but the name of the street where he lived. Songberd's Grove! "Coo, ever so pretty," said a mocking voice from somewhere, and once more a titter had run through the room. Lennie charged them like a bull. He was considerably larger and heavier than on the last occasion and did proportionately more damage. Then he went home to look at the street. Laugh at him, would they? He'd show them; there wouldn't be anything pretty about the street by the time that he had finished with it.

As though it were the class itself he charged it at a

run, breaking bottles and kicking trees, scuffing paint where he could find it and going generally berserk. At the end of the outburst he found that he had accumulated some helpers, several small and bored creatures who considered this a most wonderful game. It was then that he had the idea of getting them organised, turning Trev, Mudface and Rusty into his lieutenants as one by one they arrived to live in Songberd's Grove.

But after a bit, the pleasure of kicking things down, like that of shouting at people, palls. Lennie began to feel bored. He was growing older and went to a lot of films now; to stave off the boredom he tried a different tack. He dressed himself as much like a dandy as his limited resources would allow and tried to live in the way that he considered, from his study of the films, should go with it. He very seldom went out in person to Songberd's Grove now, but passed through it quickly on his way to more lively streets, fancying himself as the master brain who directed the Grove from behind closed doors and extracted his levy; boasting about it to the new friends that he now met, and feeling once again that now he was Somebody all right. It had all been most satisfactory until . . .

"Until now!" thought Lennie savagely, picking up the pull of the blind and letting it swing hard against the window; until this wretched red-haired boy had arrived. Things had gone wrong from the very beginning, from the moment that Martin had appeared.

He hadn't succeeded in making Martin do any work for him, and Rusty had been defeated in his mission; the next day he had told off some of the small fry to do their favourite blister-picking on the door of No. 7 and Martin, suddenly appearing, had not only helped them with it, but had said that it was just what his parents wanted, and thanked them very much. They wouldn't do it any more after that; stood to reason they wouldn't, it was no more fun.

But there was worse than that. Rusty, for the first time that anyone had done this to him for years, had given him back a cheeky answer. He'd banged him one, of course, in return, but that didn't make any difference. Mudface and Trevor, looking sidelong at him, had started to offer advice. Advice! To him, to No. 1! He ordered, he didn't take advice. And there was one thing worst of all.

Inside that boy, that wretched, skinny giggling boy, Lennie felt that there was something that was a menace and a challenge to his whole way of life, something that was not impressed by him and did not think that he was Somebody after all. He'd show him! He'd show him who was the important one, who carried the most weight here! His anger spilling over, like milk suddenly boiling, Lennie crashed open the door and went out into the row.

Where was the little runt? He had got hold of that girl too—that was another sore point in Lennie's angry mind. He himself had failed to do anything with her, the sulky little cat, but he hadn't bothered much, until he saw her and this Martin now, as thick as thieves. How had Martin got hold of her, when he hadn't been able to? What did they do with themselves all day? Like a bull swinging its head from side to side he looked up and down the empty street. What was it that Trev had said about them messing about in the garden at the back? How could he get near enough to look at them?

Dressed in his wide-shouldered, draped jacket, with narrow, drain-pipe trousers and a narrow ribbon tie which he considered the height of elegance, his long hair flopping on top of it all, he walked down the row, looking as fantastically out of proportion as if he had indeed been one of the space visitors of Martin's imagination.

He stared at the front door of No. 7, and then moved back uncertainly to No. 6. There were a lot of things you could get away with but going into somebody's else's house wasn't one of them; he walked out into the street and round the corner by their garden, heard their voices from behind the spike-

THE HEIGHT OF ELEGANCE

topped wall, and came back again. How could he get in? At that moment, as though in answer to his problem, one of the cleaning women from No. 6 turned into Songberd's Grove, staggering with the weight of her washing, which she had brought back from the Laundrette.

"Like me to carry it up for you?" It was so long since Lennie had said, or done, anything pleasant, that his intended smile came out as a kind of ghastly leer. The woman stopped and stared.

Knock her down with a feather! That dreadful boy from the end house. She dimly suspected that he was up to something, but the basket was very heavy and her feet ached. Perhaps he had turned over a new leaf.

"Wonders will never cease!" she said. "Thank you."

Lennie plodded up the stairs behind her, seized the opportunity he wanted as soon as he got to her living-room and staggered over to the window, where he dumped the stuff down.

"Nice view from here," he said vaguely, to excuse himself for standing there and looking out, and he stared angrily down into the next-door garden. The woman went into the bedroom to take off her hat and coat and did not disturb him for a moment.

There they were, the two little so-and-so's, and

the sight not only of them, but of the garden, made Lennie so furious that he wanted to throw something at them. He had determined that this row was to remain derelict and here was something that was very far from derelict; he had got all the rest of the children in the street doing what he wanted them to do and here were these two, apart and enjoying themselves, laughing and talking to each other as though he had never existed. He looked wildly round the room; he wanted to do something to them both that hurt.

But the thinking he had tried to do earlier now gave its reward; as the result of that process a glimmering of understanding came to him.

It was no good trying to do anything to them physically, even if he could find anything to throw; what he needed was to find something through which he could hurt them further inside. He stared down again to see what they were doing.

They had cleared all the stones away from the centre of the garden and left a sort of flat, trodden path of earth there; the girl was pointing downwards to it now. At the end, beyond the door out into the street, they had built a sort of fancy place and put some pot plants round it; a pile of stones, with something that looked like a face on top. Yes, it was a face, he could see it clearly now, carved on a bit of stone. As the girl stopped pointing and started demonstrating something excitably, waving her hands and dancing up and down, the boy went over to it and ran his fingers gently across the face as he was listening. It was a gesture which even Lennie recognized as one of affection, and in a minute he knew where Martin's vulnerable point was. He must get that head. As though they had read his thoughts they were draping it in something now, looking upwards from the garden. Why had they done that?

The girl was pointing to the door and had taken out a key; Martin was shaking his head; their voices floated away on a wind which was blowing in the other direction. They were going out through it! Elbowing his way past the cleaning woman who was coming in, Lennie crashed down the stairs and ran out into the street. At the far end of the row, outside No. 1, were Mudface and Trevor, and he whistled for them to come.

You couldn't get into houses, but gardens didn't count.

CHAPTER 11

"THIS AFTERNOON," Geneva was saying, as Lennie watched from above, "this very afternoon! Oh, it's like . . ." She looked around for words to express her feelings and then started off again in a flurry of gestures, ". . . like being besieged somewhere, and then suddenly hearing that relief is coming." And she looked up at the windows of the middle flat, whose occupants were at long last due.

"I don't know why you are so sure they'll be relief," muttered Martin dryly from where, with head bent and shoulders straining, he was heaving at a particularly heavy block.

"Of course they will!" But for the first time the

possibility of the new people being no help seemed to have entered Geneva's brain.

"Then we ought to finish it quickly, and get done before they come!" She darted across the garden for another stone in a renewed burst of energy. In the few days that they had been working on it they had made an amazing difference to its appearance.

Their life really *had* been rather like a siege, for the two of them had lived almost entirely at the back of the house, in the garden. Although he very much regretted the necessity and was itching to carry out a more active war, Martin had to keep reminding himself that for the moment discretion was the better part of valour, and that, although he found it extremely irksome, he must keep to this work. Once the newcomers were here and he knew which side they were on, things could start moving again; for the moment it seemed better to concentrate on getting the garden clear.

But twice every day, as well as on the occasions when he went out with his parents, Martin made it a point of honour to show himself in the front. He wasn't going to let Lennie and company think they had driven him underground. With the door open behind him for a quick retreat if necessary, he was there every morning to take the milk from the milkman and hand the empty bottles back: in the evenings, when a sprinkling of grown-ups tended to be about the Grove, gossiping and tinkering with their bicycles, and a mass attack on him by children would therefore be unlikely, he paraded solemnly twice up and down, whistling nonchalantly as he went beyond No. 4 to the further end.

Once Mudface had thrust a note at him but he had refused to take it; once Trevor, brushing by, had stuck a piece of paper in his pocket but he had dropped it out on the ground unread; so he remained ignorant of the invisible Lennie's state of mind or designs. Once Rusty had licked his lips nervously and made as if to speak to him, but Mudface had come up behind him and he had run quickly away.

On one occasion, when no grown-ups happened to be out, the three of them, Rusty between the other two, with all the crowd of small fry behind them, had slowly started to advance on him, and, until two of the Irishmen came out of No. 5 and saved the situation, it was only by thinking of Lord Simon and of his stone face in the garden that Martin managed to hold his ground.

For this face was beginning to have an extraordinary effect on him. As Martin put down the heavy stone that he was carrying, he went over to where they had enthroned it in the place of honour.

At the end of the garden, directly opposite Martin's

window, and with the path leading up to it, as Lennie had seen from above, they had built a sort of cairn of stones. Like the head, some of the pieces which Martin had kicked about on that first evening had turned out to be chips of marble and some had what seemed to be fragments of carving on them. He was beginning to think that, by the most extraordinary coincidence, this garden too, like that of Mr. Acle, must once have been a stonemason's workshop or yard.

"But years and years ago," said Geneva, when they first made the discovery, "for just look at these letters!" And that was the strangest thing of all, for beneath the base of the head, where Martin had not thought to look, were two sets of initials, first N.S. and then M.S. The edges of the letters were so worn and the capitals carved in such a curious way, with odd quirks and flourishes, that he knew they could not have been done for at least a hundred years or more. What did they mean? Was one the sculptor and the other the man whose portrait he had taken in stone? Whatever it was, the fact of their being there, and of one set of initials being Martin's own, made the head seem doubly precious and to belong to him more than ever.

"Here's another bit with some carving," said Geneva. "It looks like feathers, like a part of an angel's wing or something." And she put it down with the other worked bits beneath the face. "If only we could join them all together and make something! Who was he? He looks so confident, don't you think?" She stood back to look.

For confidence was the keynote of the stone face. From his eminence above the piled heap of rubble he laughed down at them serenely, so that even to look at him was to get new courage and to feel that everything was bound to go well. As things got worse and worse in the front of Songberd's Grove, as his mother grew more and more despondent and Martin more worried about her, he went more and more frequently to his stone friend to look at him and gain strength. In some strange way he began to feel too that not only was he working to get things right for his mother, but that he was also doing something that this man wanted him to do, and that he was their ally. A sudden thought struck him.

"They'll be able to see him from the middle flat," he said doubtfully to Geneva, as he put his hand on the face, running his fingers over its strong contours. "He'll be looking straight up at them. I don't think he ought, do you?"

Geneva shook her head violently. "No," she said, "he is only for us. We must cover him, undo him when we want to talk to him. We could make it a sort of secret ceremony!" And her eyes shone, for secrets and mystery were the breath of life to her.

Going back into the house, Martin produced a sack which had been left over by the removal men and put it tenderly over the head, weighting its loose edges down with stones. Then, turning back to the garden, he surveyed their handiwork.

As Lennie had seen from above, the earth down the middle was now flat, raked and bare. Along the side walls small heaps of stones were arranged in as orderly a manner as possible, and already the leaves of a little, vine-like creeper, as if trying to help, were beginning to sprout up from among them. La Golondrina's herb garden flourished at the foot of the balcony and its vivid colour looked lost among so much grey and brownness.

"If only we could get a bit more green somewhere," said Martin, remembering Aunt Emmeline's grass, so neat that it looked like an artificial grass mat. "I suppose we couldn't possibly make a lawn?" For a moment he toyed wildly with the idea of pulling up tufts of grass wherever he saw them and of transplanting them here.

"We could sow some grass," said Geneva, and thought for a moment. "We could put it in now. Spring and early autumn, those are the times: I read it once on a packet when my mother was buying some of her seeds. Early autumn is now. Oh, do let's get some, this minute! Then we can put it in and, whatever happens, nothing in the world can stop it coming up. It only takes about ten days to begin to show." She ran half-way to the garden gate and drew out the key.

Martin looked at the money in his pocket; there seemed to be enough. Then he looked doubtfully at the gate. He had never yet gone out that way, and it was strongly against his principles to do so now.

"Oh, I know," cried Geneva impatiently, not sharing his scruples in the least, "but surely for once it doesn't matter. We'll have to be as quick as we possibly can if we are going to get it sown before this afternoon, and the shop is round this way. You know how much we have to do!"

For the afternoon and the arrival and reception of the newcomers their plans were all made. La Golondrina had baked all the strange-looking foods and cakes which Geneva had demanded, but the table was not yet laid nor the room ready. It was arranged that Martin should take up his station out in the front early after lunch, to intercept them when they came. Realising the urgency of the situation, he reluctantly nodded his head.

"All right," he said, and the key was in the lock.

Geneva skipped out first and stood looking up and

down the side street as Martin followed her. For a moment, as he turned the key behind him, he also stood looking; then everything happened at once.

"Got 'em!" cried a voice from the top corner of the street. "Get that key quick, Alan." And as Martin tried to wrench it from the door, Mudface and Trevor came dashing down towards them.

"Quick!" For a moment, as though he were in a nightmare, Martin's feet seemed to be glued down to the pavement; then suddenly he got the key out and ran after Geneva. She knew her way and he did not, so he followed her unquestioningly.

In a pitched battle the lightness of Martin and Geneva would have told against them, but here it stood them in good stead. Proving herself to be truly the daughter of La Golondrina, Geneva skimmed like a blown leaf down the streets and round the corners, and Martin, finding a speed that he never knew he possessed, followed as though he were joined to her with a wire. But all the streets which they turned into were long ones and always, by the time they had reached the far end the two boys were in sight at the other.

They turned into a mews and went clattering over its cobbled stones; rushed over a pedestrian crossing just in the nick of time, and were on a bridge. To his surprise, for he had hardly been outside Songberd's

Grove and knew nothing of the neighbourhood, Martin saw water beneath them, and barges drawn up along a grassy bank.

"If only we could get down there among them and hide!" Geneva panted. "They might think we had gone on and over!" But before they reached the path which led downwards, the others, running parallel to them, and on the other side of the canal, came into view.

"Oh . . . I've got a stitch . . ." Geneva's breath was beginning to fail her at last. With a final effort she dashed along the far bank and turned back across the next bridge again; beyond it were trees which might give cover, growing in the garden of an old, deserted house, down by the canal side.

"Look!" They were panting along beside the garden, whose wall had been destroyed in places and was propped up now with sheets of iron: between two such sheets Martin suddenly saw a gap. Reversing their progress, he slipped in between them first and pulled Geneva through after him. They flung themselves down flat behind the fence and the iron sheets had only just stopped quivering when Mudface and Trevor went dashing past. Luckily two other children of about the same size as Martin and Geneva, running for natural and peaceful purposes, had just doubled the end of the road, and the two boys from Songberd's Grove followed them.

For a few moments Geneva and Martin did nothing but lie and draw in breath, painfully at first and then with the most exquisite satisfaction. Then they cautiously sat up and took stock of their situation.

"We'd better get away from the road a bit, hadn't we?" whispered Geneva, but Martin was looking around.

"Wait a minute," he said, and picking up an abandoned coil of wire and some brushwood that was lying about, he stuffed them into the gap through which they had come so that it no longer looked like one. Then they went on tiptoe down towards the canal.

The place in which they found themselves was, for London, quite extraordinary, and they looked round in astonishment, fascinated. It was as though by that sideways movement through the fence they had managed to transfer themselves from one world into another, entirely different; out of a slummy town and into the country, which neither of them knew. It seemed to them like a fairy-tale. All round them and above, trees shimmered and trembled in the light that was reflected from the canal water, shedding every now and then leaves which floated and turned through the air like golden feathers. Some fell on the vivid grass beneath the trees and some on the different, bottle-glass green of the water, almost dizzying the already-dazed children with the continual movement of their falling brilliance. Through the tree trunks showed the walls of an old house, down by the water's edge, and beyond it was floating a swan, completely reflected. Geneva caught her breath.

"There's cover all round," said Martin with satisfaction, looking at the thick fringe of trees and seeing them from an entirely different point of view. "I don't think we can be seen from anywhere. Well, what are we going to do?" With the chequered sunlight falling on his glasses and autumn-leaf-coloured hair, he gazed down towards the house.

"Do you suppose there is anybody in it?" asked Geneva in awe. "It looks very deserted." And she too, with her black hair streaming and her dress all caught up with leaves, looked less like a London child than a dryad who might have come out of one of the trees.

"Only one way to find out," said Martin, and started walking down towards it, over the long, thick grass that gave under his feet like a cinema carpet and was quite unlike Aunt Emmeline's scrubby stuff.

A few paces behind him, ready to turn and flee if anyone should appear, Geneva followed.

It was a splendid house, with white pillars, lofty walls and wide windows, over all of which the watery, leafy sunlight played. Steps led down from the front of it to the water, and though the ceilings of some of the rooms were down and left them open to the sky, it did not in any way detract from their beauty but rather enhanced it. Geneva was staring in fascination at a chimney-place with a green carpet of grass in front of it and weeds poking up through the grate and beside the rusty poker when Martin suddenly pulled her arm.

"Look!"

Not all the ceilings were down, and at one side of the house where they were still intact there was a long and many-windowed room. Martin pointed inside. There was furniture there of a sort and it was evidently lived in—a divan with some rugs on it, a table and a couple of chairs stood about it. But dominating the whole room was a large easel; canvases were stacked round the walls and there seemed to be brushes and palettes everywhere. Nobody was there. Advancing a little closer, Martin and Geneva flattened their noses against the glass.

"They haven't been gone long, whoever it is," said

Geneva. "There's some bread——" And suddenly she stopped in the middle of what she was going to say, turned and looked at Martin with enormous eyes.

"Bread. That's what's wrong with me. Martin, I'm nearly dead of hunger, aren't you?"

He nodded. A longing for the bubble-and-squeak which his mother, who was out, had left for him, rose up and filled his whole being; while Geneva, with anguish just as great, thought of her own wilder and more highly spiced brew. They stood there with their nostrils quivering and mouths watering.

"There is cheese there too," said Geneva, "and butter. Martin, we could pay for it afterwards. . . . We—the fact is I've just got to get in!"

Martin nodded. With hunger-sharpened eyes he could even see the crumbs on the plate now. The man, or woman, or whoever it was, had obviously eaten and gone away, so they could return the food later. It was lucky he hadn't bought the grass seed and still had some money. He moved round the window.

"Not even locked!" he said, turned the knob of the glass door and stepped inside.

Geneva made a few skating steps on the polished surface of the floor, slid across to the table and cut herself a thick slice of bread.

"New!" Her mouth full, she pushed the half loaf towards Martin. They took slice after slice and very soon the loaf was gone and the two of them, feeling very comfortably full, sat looking at each other from the two chairs into which they had sunk.

Realising that their brief moment of relaxation must soon be over, Martin heaved a profound sigh as he looked round the room. That was the worst of all this stupid business—there was never time to do anything you wanted, and how typical now it was to find himself in a fascinating place like this without time to enjoy it!

"We'll have to go out and get them some more food. Do you think Trevor and Mudface will still be hanging about outside?"

Geneva shook her head. "They'll have gone home to dinner." She knew the habits of Songberd's Grove, and nobody missed their midday meal there if they could help it. "I should think they will hang about outside the Grove—one at the front entrance and one at the back—after all, they know we shall have to come back sometime. We shall be like animals trying to get back to our holes!" she added dramatically. "And when we do come they'll try and get the key from us." She looked nervously at Martin. Trevor and Mudface, as she well knew, as long as nobody was looking, would be no respecters of size or sex.

"Even if we hid the key somewhere it wouldn't help because they wouldn't know and they would search us just the same," said Martin. "No, somehow we've got to find someone to go in with."

"Perhaps I could faint," suggested Geneva hopefully, "so that a policeman would take us?" Suiting the action to the words she flung herself backwards across the chair, rolling her eyes upwards and opening her mouth in a most life-like imitation.

"Take you to a hospital or a lunatic asylum more likely, if you look like that. Couldn't we go to the theatre where your mother works and go home with her? My father's on late tonight and my mother is probably back by now."

"And wait till ten o'clock?" asked Geneva. "Oh dear, if only we could think of someone who was quite certainly going there this afternoon. This afternoon—Martin!" She sprang out of her chair and stood facing him, her face as white as though she were actually about to faint.

"This afternoon, Thursday afternoon, the one we have been waiting for. How could we have forgotten? They will be arriving any minute now and we——"

Amidst the wreckage of all their careful plans, in

someone else's totally strange studio, they stared at each other in despair.

And at that moment they heard a footstep outside the window.

CHAPTER 12

Several years earlier, as two names had been read out from somewhere in the middle of a school register, two small boys with the same initials had giggled, been punished together and thereby become friends for the rest of their lives.

John Pim and John Pollard, and they had more in common than their initials. All through their school career the two names, as though weighted with lead, had bobbed about together at the bottom of the form list, mainly because the two boys' heads were already full of ideas which seemed to them far more important than those which the schoolmasters were trying to stuff into them. They both spent all their time drawing.

John Pim was a very small and thin boy who fizzed and spluttered about like a jumping firework when he became enthusiastic about anything, and John Pollard was stocky and square and well-covered. But as though they had to make up somewhere for their respective shapes, John Pim only drew curving and flourishing and circular things while John Pollard did all his pictures in mazes of spidery lines which looked as though he had scratched them with a pin.

After he left school John Pollard decided to take to portrait painting and achieved such astonishing and unusual likenesses to people with his pin-point lines that he very soon became an enormous success, particularly among very fat women, who were flattered by having their portraits done in this way.

John Pim, only really at home when he was surrounded by smooth and curving surfaces, became first an architect and then an expert on the restoration of church monuments and spent his time wandering happily about among them, tenderly feeling marble cherubs, stone duchesses and periwigged statesmen for the first signs of decay. The two Johns, very little changed since the days when they had first sniggered together at school, and secretly finding life a little dull now that they had left it, had somehow managed to stick to each other and had eventually set up house together in London.

Walking along gloomily one day by the canal and wishing that he had never started portrait-painting, because the fat women wouldn't leave him alone and were always ringing up or banging on the door of his studio, wishing that he had at least some private place to live where they couldn't find him, John Pollard suddenly thought he saw one pursuing him from the opposite side of the road and slipped in a panic through the identical gap which Martin and Geneva had used. Like them he had discovered the house by the water and come to the conclusion that it would suit him better than any other place in the world. The agent had been willing to let it and had given him the key to a more seemly way in; meaning to mend the gap but never having done so, he and John Pim moved in and lived there in secrecy, keeping the other studio for official purposes.

Today, having just finished a most successful drawing of a really enormous woman, done in a bird's nest of fragile lines, John Pollard was wandering home in a state of depression and feeling very hungry, as he always did after working; he was thinking how little excitement there was in life nowadays and how pleasant it would be to paint something thin and vivid and moving for a change. Lost in his thoughts, he went absent-mindedly in by the old gap, kicked the brushwood and the coil of wire to one side without noticing them and walked over the grass to the studio, thinking, above everything else, how tired he was of bread and cheese. In order to keep the privacy of their canal-house they had no one to work for them there and neither of them could cook. Sighing, he put his hand to the door, and looked up.

On the other side of the glass, staring at him in open-mouthed horror, were a boy and a girl. The boy's hair was red and he had very round glasses; the girl's hair was long and black and her eyes were almost as round naturally. Wondering for one distracted moment if he had been working too hard and was seeing things through hunger, John Pollard opened the door gingerly and went in. He put out a finger and touched one of the children. It was real.

"We . . ." they both began.

He raised his eyebrows and looked at them, then pushed them aside. It was tiresome to find them there and sooner or later there would have to be some explanations but for the moment his main and all-absorbing interest lay beyond them, on the table. Once he had eaten he felt he could deal with the situation; he looked for the food. The loaf, the cheese and the butter were gone.

"Where's my lunch?" he said angrily and the

whole scene suddenly seemed ridiculously like the story of the three bears.

"We . . . we thought that you had had it," said the red-haired boy. "There were crumbs, you see, and it looked as though someone had eaten. We were very hungry; we were going to buy some more and put it back . . ."

"You were hungry, were you?" said John Pollard, staring at him fiercely. "Well, so am I hungry. Enormously, vastly, inconceivably hungry. And as it happens, the crumbs were from breakfast, so your deductions were wrong. We have bread and cheese for breakfast and lunch and tea here, and often for supper too." And because that was the thought that had been upsetting him all the way home, he glared at them afresh.

"Oh, but this is terrible!" Geneva, who had inherited all her mother's reverence for food, forgot everything else. She clasped her hands in distress as she looked at him. His expression changed from anger to bewilderment.

"I know—look!" Forgetting that they were intruders and for all he knew criminals, that their presence there had somehow to be explained away, Geneva took a quick step forward in her concern and put a hand on his arm. "We were going out to buy some more cheese and some bread to put back

J. P.

for you, but now I will go and buy you better things than that, proper things, and cook them for you. There is a stove? There is a shop I know on the corner, and while I am gone . . . Martin, you explain!" Her eyes danced at having evaded this awkward moment, and before anyone had time to speak she was out of the room and away. John Pollard blinked.

"Has she got any money?" he asked, and sat weakly down. "Well, perhaps, as she suggested," he went on, "you had better explain."

Standing and blinking down at the man in front of him, Martin made about three false starts; then it seemed easier to start at the very beginning and he did so, from the arrival of their furniture van at Songberd's Grove. As he spoke, John Pollard's listlessness vanished and he sat forward in his chair.

"Good heavens, what an extraordinary story!" he said, when Martin had done. "Well, of course that explains why you had to come in here." As Martin flushed with relief Pollard eyed him closely. From the telling of the story, although it had been done in the simplest of possible words, there had emerged a spirit of independence and a determination not to be messed about with that had endeared Martin to him considerably. He also felt pleasantly as though he were back in his own schooldays again.

"And these people are coming this afternoon, are

they?" he mused. "Reinforcements, but nobody knows for which side. What'll they be like?" He frowned and to Martin's surprise seemed to be just as much occupied with the question as he and Geneva were themselves.

"Well, of course I can come back with you when you go so that you get the key in safely," he went on reflectively, "but that still doesn't get you much further, does it?"

Martin shook his head. The relief of being able to talk about what he felt, and to someone whose mind seemed to work in the same way as his, was so great that he felt he must try and put into words the thing that had been worrying him since the very beginning.

"The trouble is," he said, frowning down at the ground as he tried to put it exactly, "to think how to deal with them."

He looked up at John Pollard, blinked and went on again in a rush.

"I mean, they get what they want by breaking everything, by pinching and kicking and hurting people, frightening the small ones and spoiling everybody's houses, and—short of having police all round them all the time—the only way to stop them doing it seems to get enough people to do exactly the same back at them, only worse. Only, if you did that . . ." He looked up again, for this was the bit that really bothered him and he didn't know if he could explain.

"If you do, you're doing the same thing as they are, and you are just as bad as they are and doing the very thing that you were fighting against, and so even if you beat them, it's really they who have won in the end." Was there any hope that this man could understand, when it wasn't even very clear to himself?

John Pollard understood very well indeed. "You seem to be touching lightly on one of the world's greatest problems," he said dryly, and at this moment Geneva, with her hands full, came bursting in through the French window.

In her family, cooking seemed to be inseparable from colour. Even to put in an omelette she had found bits of red things and green things and some of a curious purply brown. A small bottle of olive oil stuck out from under one arm and once she had put that, and the precious eggs down, she let everything slide onto a table and looked anxiously at Martin. It had cost their last penny, but she had felt that she must not skimp her art.

"A pan?" she said, "and some matches? A knife?" And as John Pollard gave her the very battered and limited equipment of his kitchen she got to work. Martin watched her with interest. Geneva cooking was a new and dedicated Geneva whom he had not seen before.

His own mother produced good, solid and appetising food but she did it rather absent-mindedly, as though the same well-tried mixtures had produced the same results for so long there was no reason to think that they would ever do anything else. It was the future of her pans that she really had at heart; she was always longing for the moment when the food could be emptied out of them and they be cleaned as bright as lighthouse windows again and put back on their shelves.

Aunt Emmeline cooked distastefully, with her finger tips, as though she were too fine and rare a soul to have to deal with such coarse and earthy things as food; she really much preferred ready-cooked meals which came out of tins and packets, without any trouble to her. These were the only two experiences of cooking that he had had, but Geneva!

She shook the oil into the pan and peered into it with an expression of intense concentration so that her face over the blue smoke looked like a young witch's. She washed and pared the bright-coloured things into delicate shreds and tossed each one in as though she were muttering a different incantation for it, and with each a new and appetising smell rose on the air. When all was ready she broke in the eggs, turned the creaming yellow once or twice with a fork and shook them a little, turned half of the omelette over so that it made a perfect, brown-edged semi-circle, whisked it out of the frying-pan and placed it, smoking with heat and light as sea-foam, in front of John Pollard. Sniffing the air unbelievingly and looking almost as though he could cry he gazed down at it in awe.

He was just about to take up his fork, his mouth watering shamefully, when there was a rattle at the window and another man walked in.

He was a small and very thin man with thick, wild hair and bright eyes. He looked at Martin and Geneva like a startled rabbit, started to say something and then suddenly sniffed too. With a most curious expression on his face he looked down towards where John Pollard was taking the first forkful of omelette.

"Oh, really, J. Pim," said John Pollard tetchily, "what a moment to arrive! Oh, all right, I suppose I shall have to give you some too." And cutting off a portion that was much less than half, he motioned to Geneva for a plate and slid it over to him, eating the edges of his own piece quickly to reduce it to equal size so that its bigness shouldn't show.

The smaller man nibbled at his precisely, but with no less enjoyment.

"I could make another," said Geneva, "if I had some more eggs."

They looked at her longingly for a moment, then John Pollard shook his head.

"No," he said regretfully, "it would take too long and we have got other things to do. Do you always cook like this?"

"It is nothing to my mother," said Geneva modestly.

"Your mother? Then your mother is a cook?"

"My mother is a dancer," said Geneva simply and superbly; "she is La Golondrina."

"Would someone mind explaining?" said the little man wildly. "I'm getting bewildered."

John Pollard threw his hands up in the air and let them fall slap on his knees again.

"You may well ask, J. Pim," he said, "but first, let us all introduce ourselves. Martin Singer, you said, didn't you?" He turned towards Martin, who nodded, "and this proudly named girl seems to be simply Geneva. I am John Pollard," he went on, "and this is John Pim, who is an architect." He turned towards his friend.

"I found them here when I got back from Mrs. Porterhouse's sitting this morning," he said. "They were being chased and had come in through the gap, as I did. Owing to the chase they were very hungry and as they thought that we had eaten they took our bread and cheese, but were handsomely prepared to replace it. When I came in the lady Geneva—" he bowed towards her—"offered to make me an omelette. You had half the result."

"I wouldn't say quite half," corrected John Pim mildly, "but why were they being chased?"

"Because in the street where they live some toughs have set up a sort of dictatorship, and because Martin and Geneva won't take it; because they want to turn the row into a pleasant place and not a slum and because they want to be left in peace. Because in short, J. Pim, they are absolutely right about it and we've got to do something to help them!" He thumped his fist down on the table, and, as though they were back at school again, went on to tell John Pim all the details of the war of Songberd's Grove.

"And these new people are coming this afternoon, did you say?" said the thin man, jumping up. "Well, then, why aren't we there?"

CHAPTER

13

"TERRIBLE FIGHTER J. Pim is," said John Pollard complacently. "Like a bull-dog—never knows when to let go." He and Martin were sitting in the back of John Pim's small car, behind John Pim's narrow body, and speeding dangerously towards Songberd's Grove.

Martin fidgeted and looked out of the window. Sensing that something was wrong, John Pollard looked across at him.

"The thing is . . ." Martin started uneasily. "Well, to make it lasting we've still got to do any fighting ourselves. I mean, it's awfully kind of you, but you and Mr. Pim are still grown-ups . . ."

In the excitement of the last hour John Pollard had almost forgotten this, but he saw Martin's point.

"All right, old chap, we won't butt in. Not until you need us, that is. It's your war and you are making the plans. But don't forget that the studio is at your disposal whenever you want, as well as the car; not to mention the strength and the sinews of J. Pim and J. Pollard, such as they are."

Feeling, after the magnanimity of this offer that he was guilty of the most enormous ingratitude, Martin swallowed, looked round at his friend again and for the second time tried to explain.

"It—you see, if they see us with you all the time they'll think that we're afraid and daren't come out alone. If we won anything with you there it . . . it wouldn't be a proper win, not permanent. . . ." His voice trailed off, then he started again. "I mean, we've got to do it this time to get in with the key, and it's awfully good of you to help us, and if we can come to the studio and talk to you sometimes . . ." He also thought longingly of the sheets of paper and the pencils there as he looked at John Pollard. Oh, why had all this tiresome business cropped up and spoilt everything!

"That's all right." John Pollard touched his knee for a moment as though to seal a bargain. "And call on us when you want us. Perhaps," he added hopefully, "the lady Geneva might even be persuaded to come and cook a meal for us every now and again?"

Hearing her name, Geneva turned round from the front with a dazzling smile, looked forward again and cried out, "Here we are," as the huddled grey row came into sight. The only splash of colour was one of her mother's shawls, hung out of a corner of one window and obliterating the name of the row.

"What shall we do, then?" asked John Pim, turning round to Martin as they pulled up in the street outside. "Shall we both come in?"

"One's enough," said John Pollard firmly from the back. "You go, J. Pim. Pretend you're an inspector of drains or something, but don't let anyone get hold of that key. Who's got it, by the way?"

"Geneva," said Martin.

"Then stick close to her. Good-bye now and good luck to you, see you again soon. I'll be leaning over the hedge to watch." And as they thanked him and slid out of the car quickly, Geneva, Martin and J. Pim started on their walk to the door.

Inside the hedge, like the wrack left on a beach after high tide, the ground seemed to be littered with odds and ends not yet dealt with by the removal men. The small fry, as they had been on the day of Martin's arrival, were grouped silently about, and people came and went through the doorway of No. 7.

Martin looked up at Trevor and Mudface, who were approaching him with assumed expressions of false friendliness. Well, Geneva had the key; if she went on with John Pim all would be well. He dropped back a little to meet them.

"Jolly good game, that was, eh, that we had just now?" said Trevor, leering, and in a raised voice so that the grown-ups could hear him: "Shall we do it again?" Before Martin realised what was happening, the two of them suddenly started clapping their hands all over him, feeling in every pocket for the possible shape of a key. With one final stroke Trevor raised his hand to switch off Martin's glasses but Martin's had been expecting this and got in a resounding smack on Trevor's face first, then he ducked and ran.

But Mudface was before him and was between him and Geneva, just on the doorstep.

"Here you, I've got a message for you: your mother's been taken queer." He plucked at Geneva's sleeve and, as she turned, suddenly grabbed hold of her arms. "She's down along here." Oh, what was J. Pim doing, allowing this, thought Martin in anguish, unable to get to her in time.

"Oh no, she's not," cried Geneva, "she's at the theatre!" and lowered her head. There was a wild yell from Mudface as she bit and for a moment Martin had almost a fellow-feeling for him. Then he grinned as he saw Mudface looking down at the reddening circle on his arm and Geneva ran indoors.

"Don't forget to disinfect it, chum," he said, as he prepared to follow her, and John Pim, who had been standing in a sort of trance, looking up at the house, and overdoing a little, thought Martin, his role of inspector, came back to earth.

"Eh?" he said, blinking. "You've both got in all right? Good, then, we'll see you again soon." Smiling at them briefly he started backing away towards the roadway, still looking up at the house. He backed into the removal men, apologised, rounded the corner backwards, still moving crabwise, and sank back-first into the car.

"Do you see those houses, J. Pollard," he asked dazedly, "and the state they have been allowed to get into? Do you see those fanlights, those arches and the shape of those windows? Where have those children brought us to? I can't see the name anywhere. It seems to me we've stumbled on one of the perfect early Georgian rows in London!"

"Well, that's that," said Martin, once they were in, but Geneva, with her finger on her lips stood stock-still in the hall.

"They're here," she said, for the last furniture man

had now left, and from above came a murmur of voices. They listened anxiously, but there seemed to be no sounds of small children or babies.

"Ssh," said Martin warningly.

The people who were speaking had evidently come out from their room and onto the landing; one voice was low and sounded like a girl's, and the other was familiar.

"Rusty," said Martin, but before he had time to say any more there was a nervous rush and clatter of boots down the stairs and Rusty himself was there and staring at them with a very odd expression.

His round blue eyes were opened to their fullest, as though he had seen something quite extraordinary and he was still blinking a little, as though the something had been very bright. His whole face was pursed up almost to bursting point with the astonishment and importance of what he had just seen. Forgetting for the moment that they were enemies and seeing them only as someone to share his feelings with, he burst into speech.

"Oh, gee!" he said. Then he suddenly realised where he was, looked round the forbidden territory of their hall in panic and, with a sound somewhere between a gasp and a giggle, fled out through the door and into the road.

"Well, what does that mean?" said Geneva, and they looked at each other.

Martin put one foot on the bottom of the stairs, blinked and cleared his throat.

"Better get it over," he said.

Side by side they started upwards, moving a little more slowly on each stair. Whatever could Rusty have seen to make him look like that? On the landing above they paused outside the door.

"None of it's ready! Nothing's tidy!" whispered Geneva in sudden panic.

"Doesn't matter. The food's there—that's the main thing." Martin had lifted his hand. The knock seemed enormously loud, echoing up and down the stairs.

"What if the parents come?" Geneva was close against Martin's side.

"Ask for the children of course." But footsteps were already coming towards the door. It opened and it was as though a flood of light had come out for a moment; Martin's eyes took on the same dazzled expression that Rusty's had done. There stood in the doorway the most astonishingly beautiful creature that he had ever seen.

It was a girl, older and taller than himself and Geneva, but still not grown-up, and everything about

THE NEW GIRL

her seemed to shine. On that dusty landing the dust-laden sunlight lit up the heavy locks of corn-coloured hair that fell round her head, and seemed to shine through the milky whiteness of her skin and in her sea-blue eyes. She looked at them with mild inquiry; there was a note, Lennie's, which she had evidently just been reading, in her hand.

"Please?" she said, and her voice was soft and foreign.

Martin took a breath and moistened his lips, but before he could say anything Geneva suddenly tugged at his arm, moving in front of him quickly as he fell back a little. She stuck up her chin in the air.

"I am sorry," she said, with freezing dignity, "we have made a mistake." And to Martin's total astonishment, before he could think or protest, she started dragging him away up the stairs.

The girl looked at them for a moment, puzzled, shrugged and made a little gesture with her hand, and then went and shut the door. When there was nothing but blank wood in the place where her astonishing presence had been, Martin turned to Geneva in bewilderment.

"What was all that in aid of?" he asked.

"Come upstairs." Her voice was at its fiercest. She opened the door and Martin followed her into *The Arabian Nights* room, where, on the table, the cakes and the sweets for their tea-party were waiting to be put out on plates. Like a fury Geneva swept round the room, throwing open the windows, jerking at the shawls on the furniture and hitting the gaudy cushions as though they were personal enemies; then by the table she stopped and for the first time looked up.

"She is no good!" she said.

Martin looked at her in astonishment. Admittedly he himself had not thought the new girl much of a fighting type; he doubted whether she would be much active help to them, but at the same time she had seemed pleasant enough. Surely she could be a passive ally if not an active one? He looked at Geneva.

"All that yellow!" she said disgustedly. "All that white! Like a turnip! And you goggling at her there!" Turning quickly down to the table so that her own coal-black locks fell over her face, she picked up one of her mother's pastries, which was to have been the centre-piece of the party, and stared at it. Suddenly she hurled it down onto the floor in a fury, so that it broke into a thousand flakes; then she burst into tears.

"Go away!" she said, and Martin made a thankful and hasty exit, running down the stairs and past the landing where lived the source of all this trouble.

Girls! He shook his head as he got out of the

danger zone and back into his own territory. You never knew where you were with them. You could spend a day with them, just as he had with Geneva today, sharing work, danger and excitement in an effortless companionship, and then suddenly, out of the blue, this! He felt thankful for the new friends he had made that day and to think that there were at least two safe and predictable male creatures in this bewildering new London world. To get things back in their right place in his mind again he felt that he must go and commune with the face in the garden, something which was utterly and exclusively masculine.

But he was not able to get straight through to it. He went in by the sitting-room door to see if his parents were back and found that they were both standing by the window, a letter in his mother's hand. She looked up at him with a frown of worry and concentration.

"Your Aunt Emmeline," she said, and needed to say no more.

"When?" Martin's heart sank.

"Next week. Tuesday. Says she has just got time to pop in and see us before she goes up north. Pop!" Mrs. Singer's face expressed her scorn. For the peering, prying, calculatingly critical visit which her sister-in-law obviously intended, pop was indeed an inadequate word. Then her expression changed to one of extreme resolution.

"We're going to get that door painted," she said. "With a week-end in front of us, there's just time. Look, your father has bought the paint."

But, although he admired it duly and briefly as Mr. Singer held up the tin, for once Martin was unable to appreciate such glorious redness. This was a situation which demanded every atom of his thought and concentration. It was essential that he be alone.

He turned through his room, out over the balcony and into the garden, then ran down its length and to the piece of sacking at the end. He twitched it aside and looked for the familiar, friendly and strength-giving features, but only the round leather blank of a burst football stared back at him.

Someone had taken his precious face away and put this object in its place. As he went back to the sitting-room in answer to a call from his mother he banged the ball down in the hall hatstand in disgust.

CHAPTER 14

As SOON as Trevor and Mudface had returned at lunch-time, reporting that Martin and Geneva had gone into hiding somewhere, that they still had the key and had locked the garden gate behind them before they left, Lennie went into action. Finishing his meal rapidly he told his two henchmen to swallow theirs double-quick too and join him out in the front of the houses, so that they could keep a watch on the two entrances. It all went, in fact, just as Geneva had predicted, except that as by a curious coincidence all the mothers in the Grove that day had chanced to provide good lunches for their offspring, resentment against this hurrying of good food was added to their general score against Martin.

Still wearing his latest, most draped and longest jacket, Lennie prowled up and down the empty row and considered ways and means. How could you get into a closed garden with spikes along its wall, through a house with a locked front door? He knew that the plan of No. 7 was the same as that of his own house, so he would know exactly where to go if he could once get through that door. As everyone knew the exact timetable of everyone else in Songberd's Grove, he knew too that the old tailor was probably inside. Slowly, as he tried to think of a plausible way of getting in, the neighbouring doors opened and one by one the gorged and early-lunched small fry came trickling back into the row.

As a herd of small deer might look at some large and dangerous animal at a water-hole, they looked at Lennie with apprehension. Two of them had with them their greatest treasure, a punctured football discarded by someone's elder brother, and with it they were going to try and fulfill their greatest ambition—to play a real game. They too knew the Grove's timetable; Mudface and Trevor, who had a habit of confiscating balls as soon as they saw them, were not usually about at this time, and the sight of Lennie himself was a rare and terrifying one nowadays. The one who was holding the ball dropped it nervously, and the sound brought him to Lennie's attention.

"A ball, eh?" asked Lennie with ghastly good humour. He had a feeling, quite new to him, that for the moment diplomacy would serve him better than brute force. If he just took the ball away from them now, at this moment, they would set up such a howling that probably all their mothers would come out, and he wanted their ball very badly. For the second time that day he tried out his smile. To him this time it seemed to go more easily, but the results on the small fry were not reassuring. One of them howled and ran back into a doorway; the others shrank a little closer together, protecting their ball.

"What are you going to play? Football? Where are the goals, then?"

As the small fry stared at him, speechless and quite paralysed, Lennie marked out two goals for them in the mud, still keeping an anxious eye on No. 7 as he walked up and down.

"Now." Dividing them into two groups with his hand, as though they had been a netful of minnows, he sent some of them to one end and some to the other. "I'll be goalie on this side. All right, start playing!"

With feeble and ineffectual kicks, casting nervous glances at Lennie in the goal and not enjoying themselves at all, the small creatures rushed backwards and forwards like mechanical figures in a slot machine while Lennie bided his time with impatience. Eventually, as it slipped between two pairs of shaking hands, the ball came trickling down towards him, in the goal outside No. 7. Making a great show of defending the goal and rushing forth to meet it with loud cries, Lennie turned and kicked it as if by accident over the side wall into the street.

"Stay where you are. I'll get it!" He ran out after it and disappeared round the side wall of the row. It was the work of a moment to punt it over the wall and into the garden of No. 7.

"Gone into the garden," he explained to the children as he came back, leaving them to work out for themselves the astonishing flight of a ball which could make a right-angled turn. "Don't worry, I'll get it for you!" As they huddled anxiously in the road behind him he rang at No. 7's bell.

After an interval the door opened and Mr. Triplett stood blinking at him in the doorway.

"These kids have sent their ball over into your garden," said Lennie. "Can I get it for them?"

The old man, staring at Lennie and obviously thinking of something else, nodded, and before he could say anything Lennie was down the passage, out through Martin's room and into the garden, looking with disgust at its tidyness as he passed. If only he had time to mess the whole thing up properly! But the stone head was his main objective and time was precious. Holding the ball under one arm, he removed the sack.

The face gave him a shock. From where he had seen it from upstairs he hadn't realised that the thing was quite so lifelike, but this was no time or place for fancy thoughts. Sticking the football in its place because he couldn't carry both, and covering it over with the sack again, he put the heavy head under his coat, where it bulged exactly like a ball, and staggered back to the house with it, up the steps and into Martin's room.

Once again he looked round him with loathing, thinking of what he would like to do, but the head, growing heavier every minute now, was nearly breaking his arms. He stumbled out into the passage and bumped into Mr. Triplett, who put out a wavering hand to detain him. Well, it was no good risking anything now; for the third time Lennie was forced to give his caricature of a smile.

The old man did not even notice. Shaking his head and with an expression of extreme sorrow he lifted his hand and started to feel Lennie's shoulders; mysteriously produced a tape measure which he ran along them, and sighed. Feeling as though his arm muscles were being dragged out by the roots, Lennie shifted from foot to foot and stared down at him. Whatever was the old beezer going to do?

"Exactly the same width as his Lordship's," said Mr. Triplett, looking up at Lennie and shaking his head reproachfully. "I thought they were, saw it in a minute, as you went down the passage. And you wear a thing like that!" Letting his hands fall to the edge of Lennie's garment, which he would not grace by the name of coat, he twitched at the cheap and bright blue stuff with a disdain beyond words and then let it fall again. As one who had seen the ultimate in distastefulness, he turned, still shaking his head, and went back into his room.

Lennie staggered out through the door, to the audience of expectant small fry whom he had completely forgotten. Furious with them, with Mr. Triplett and with his new blue suit, as well as with the weight of the monstrous thing under his arm, he took it out on them, barged the nearest ones away with his shoulder and tottered down the row to No. 1, as the children, howling for their lost ball, ran straggling along beside him.

Once inside, Lennie dumped the thing down on his bed, stood massaging his arms for a minute or two and then turned to look at it.

From among the blankets where it had fallen, the

face looked back at him. In a sudden burst of fury Lennie snatched up the nearest object he could find, which was a wooden shoe-tree, and brought it down across the face. The shoe-tree splintered, but the face remained serenely the same. Lennie looked wildly round and tried everything in sight on it; his weapons bent and cracked and his hands stung, but the features still smiled at him unmoved.

This thing was beginning to get under his skin and give him the shivers. He stopped in his assault for a moment and stared at the head as it lay on the bed. To his sensitive eyes its smile seemed to be both pitying and critical now.

Pity! He'd show it! Lifting it with both hands he held it as high above his head as he could and crashed it down on the floor, hoping to break its nose, deface or humiliate it in some way. The whole room trembled but it was the soft wood of the floor-boards that suffered and not the stone. Seeming to have one eyebrow raised in mockery now the face still smiled at him from where it lay sideways on the ground.

With a curious muffled sound Lennie rushed at it and wrapped it round in an old shirt, then he pushed it into the back of a cupboard and slammed the door, so that he needn't go on looking at it. But as though it had been painted with some sort of phosphorus that could shine in his mind's eye, Lennie still went on seeing it. As he strolled out to join his dashing friends and parade up and down the street with them, it was as though a slow puncture had been started in him, and his swagger and self-confidence were seeping away. Whatever he said and whatever he did, the face, like an invisible but ever-present witness, was there behind him, smiling ironically; not exactly criticising but, what was far more disturbing, inviting Lennie to criticise himself.

It was something which had never happened to him before and it nearly drove him mad.

CHAPTER

15

ON THE next day, which was Friday, the front door of No. 7 was scraped of the few shreds and tatters of paint which years of neglect and the small fry had left on it. On Saturday Mr. Singer was to give it an undercoat and on Sunday and Monday its two coats of ultimate red glory were to be painted over it, for luckily the weather was brilliantly fine and wonderful for drying. Mrs. Singer had unscrewed the lion's-head knocker and was polishing it with frenzy. Her usual calm had deserted her and she made her husband's and Martin's labours on the door a hundred times more difficult than they should have been by trying to wash the door-steps under their feet and the fanlight over their heads as they worked, darting in between them with her brush, cloth and water whenever she saw a chance. Everything else was already at perfection point within and without; the sitting-room window shone like a diamond and the stonework all round it had been scrubbed for as far as hand and arm could reach. The plants, for fear of cats, were to be put out first thing on Tuesday morning.

Looking at it all from in front with a critical eye as he stood back from the door for a minute, Martin had a disturbing feeling that these few bright spots only made all the rest of the row seem worse, attracting the eye to the dingy surroundings by the very contrast. But he shook his head and went doggedly back to work. Ever since yesterday evening he had felt as dazed as though someone had hit him hard over the back of the head. The loss of his stone face had made a yawning gap in his life and his relations with Geneva were so strained that their few encounters had been like those of two tight-rope walkers meeting in mid-air. For the sake of peace and out of a profound distrust for all women now he refused to speak to the new girl and had received several talkings-to on the subject from his usually placid mother, whose nerves were now strung to breaking point. She had found an ally and a fellow stair-scrubbing enthusiast in the newcomer's mother, who was Swiss; and Helga, with her shining white and gold cleanliness, seemed to her a far better companion for Martin than that odd, dark gypsy-looking girl.

As if he cared about either of them, the black one or the fair, at the moment! Attacking the door fiercely with his scraper again, Martin thought about his stone head. How was he to get it back? That it was Lennie who had taken it was quite obvious, but where had he put it? In his room somewhere, Martin supposed, and, in his anger, scraped down a layer too deep. His head in that room! But what was the good of thinking about it? He couldn't do anything now. He must see his mother through this business of Aunt Emmeline first; then and then only could he plan his next campaign. In a way, and a shaving of sound wood curled up behind his scraper as he took his thoughts off his work, it might even be quite a good thing. If he did nothing for a few days, Lennie might think nothing was going to happen, relax his vigilance and get careless. Masterly inactivity —Martin had heard the phrase once and it pleased him. But in the meantime, like a mother whose child had been kidnapped and who did not know how it was being treated, his heart bled for his stone friend.

"You don't want to dig at it like that!" Martin jumped. While he had been thinking, Mr. Bolsom had come out of No. 6 and was watching him at work. "Look." He went inside for a minute and came out with a scraper of his own. For the first time since the original disaster he looked at his own would-be yellow door, pulling the tool expertly down one panel. "That's the way, see," he said, but his thoughts seemed to be far away. He stood back and scratched his head.

"I've still got the paint," he said to Martin doubtfully. "Special line it was; cheap. Lovely colour, though." He pursed his lips and stood as if trying to make up his mind while Martin waited anxiously, hardly daring to hope. Was he going to take heart again and repaint his door? It seemed almost too good to be true.

"Yes. I will. I'll have another go at it," said Mr. Bolsom at length, and for the first time that afternoon Martin forgot his stone face.

As the old man went inside to get into his working clothes, Martin's thoughts brightened considerably. Two doors! And Mr. Bolsom's was certain to be well done; a professional job. If he could manage to meet Aunt Emmeline at the bus stop and lead her in at this end, talking hard all the time she approached No. 7 . . . if only he could arrange some sort of screen between No. 6 and the rest of the row. . . . He thought regretfully of the small fry and wished, for the first time, that he had devoted a little attention to winning them over. He looked down the row to where they were grouped.

The character of the small fry, had he known it, like that of a down-trodden people that has been too long put upon, was changing. All the time that Lennie had been making use of them, one or two of the older boys had, without his realising it, begun to grow out of small-fry stage, and the first slight tremors of rebellion were now trembling through their ranks. This feeling might have remained vague for a long time yet, but the stealing of their ball and the subsequent feeling of injustice had hardened it. Whenever they came out of the houses now they held amateur, untidy sorts of meetings, huddling together like sparrows round a crumb, with the two largest small boys as agitators. Only the little girls tended to stray away at the edges.

"Hallo!" Martin jumped once again. Really, he must pull himself together and collect his thoughts. It was the second time someone had come up on him without his realising it. He glared at the foreign girl whose soft voice had disturbed him.

"Hallo," he returned, still taking no risks and feeling at his most ungracious.

She looked at him as though disappointed for a moment, and then slightly shrugging her shoulders, went past him and out into the sunshine. She stood undecidedly in it for a few minutes and then, being one of those people who are irresistibly drawn towards children, moved towards the bunch of small fry.

Martin felt inexplicably guilty. As he had now got into the habit of doing in difficult moments, for guidance and reassurance that he had done right, he looked towards his inner man, but received no answer back. He even had the most curious sensation that it was laughing at him. Pushing the absurd thought out of his mind, he got back to work. Somewhere at the back of his mind, without fully registering it, he was aware of a golden-haired figure sitting down on the step of No. 5 and of the crowd of small, stray children slowly gravitating towards her like pins to a magnet. He went on working out his plans for the next three days.

Tonight there was no need to do anything, the two doors would be merely scraped; tonight he must sleep early and long because after that it didn't seem to him that he would be able to get much more sleep until after Aunt Emmeline's visit was over. Somehow—and the problem was so vast and impossible of solution that his mind shied away from it—he would have to spend all his time out here for the next three days, both by day and by night. And at a time like this he had to have this trouble with Geneva! He looked round for other possible help, saw the fair girl almost hidden in clusters of children and beyond her Rusty, his round eyes wide open, standing and staring, having been smitten to the heart. Frustrated, Martin turned back to the door and was attacking it with desperate and furious energy when he became aware that someone was moving about in the shadows of the hall behind it.

Geneva, her curiosity stronger even than her jealousy, came out. She stood looking at him for a moment without speaking, her eyes blacker and more impenetrable than ever. Also without speaking, Martin went on working. She looked at the door and then at the Bolsoms', giving a start of surprise.

"Your aunt, she is coming?" she said quickly.

"Tuesday," said Martin.

"And the door will be painted?"

"Tomorrow."

"Oh, Martin!" She came down the steps and stood beside him. "Then we shall have to take it in turn. To watch it, I mean. I suppose you have got it all worked out?" And she gazed up at him with admiring confidence. At last Martin stopped working and looked back.

It was as easy as that, it was over! Martin gave a sigh of relief and somewhere inside him something slid back into place. Extraordinary! So his troubled feeling had been just as much to do with Geneva as with the stone head. Still surprised at himself, he grinned.

Geneva's face, which had been screwed up like an anxious monkey's, relaxed, and she gave vent to an enormous sigh, the exact counterpart of Martin's.

"Then what are we going to do, Martin; how can we work it?" In her relief she was now all flattery and deference and anxiety to please. She glanced up at the window of her mother's flat.

"I'll clean our window too, and all round it," she cried. "Cleaner than anything you ever saw! I'll put flowers on the window-sill and tell my mother to be near so that she can be leaning out. Then you can tell your aunt that you live in the same house as La Golondrina," she added proudly, and glanced down the street as though she could already see Aunt Emmeline approaching. Her eyes fell on the group of children and its centre, hardened and then slid back to Martin's.

"But she really is too yellow, no?" As always when she was anxious, she became more foreign.

"Haven't bothered to look, never gave it a thought," said Martin loftily, and at these judicious words peace lapped round them in a sunny tide. He told her about the theft of the head, and plans began to form in his mind as to how to guard the doors.

"Could you stay awake indoors?" he asked and Geneva nodded, violently. To prove she was better than that yellow-headed thing she would do anything; go days without sleep, food, water; fight battalions of boys.

Martin nodded. "Good. Then this is what I thought we could do. I'll stay out there—somewhere behind that bush over by the road, I think, where I can see both doorways, and if they come I'll ring a bell. This bell." He fished a little flat one out of his pocket, holding its tongue. "It's a cow-bell, it came from Switzerland and makes quite a good noise. If I ring it hard you'll hear it, then you could go and wake my parents and tell them what's happening. All right?" Of Geneva's ability to waken even the heaviest sleepers he had no doubt.

Once again Geneva nodded.

"Coffee," she said sagely. "Coffee will keep us awake. Somebody gave my mother a pound. She has been ill, you know." To illustrate where her mother's ailment lay she graphically clasped her stomach and groaned. "I'll make a lot and put it in bottles; we'll drink it black and strong and that will keep us awake. Oh, Martin!" Her eyes dancing with excitement, the old Geneva again, she clasped her hands and looked up at the front of the house.

"I'll do it all now! Come up when you have finished."

And shortly from the window above Martin the smell of brewing coffee began to seep out, followed by a thin and narrow hand, brown against the white cloth which it clutched, wielded and shook with tremendous energy.

Feeling tired after all the physical and emotional exertions of his day, Martin stopped scraping for a moment, stood back and looked at the face of Songberd's Grove. As his room had once done, this time it seemed to look back at him.

The odd thing was that although he had thought about very little else but the Grove for the last ten days, after the first shock of his arrival he had scarcely bothered to look at it. Whether it was that you grow protective towards something that you are fighting for or whether he had just grown used to it he didn't know, but the most extraordinary thing seemed to have happened—he had grown fond of it! It seemed to him now to have just as much personality as his room and as the head.

Really it must be just because he had got used to it, but behind the dirt and disrepair, everything seemed to fit in so well; the doors were just the right height and size beneath their fanlights, the arches curving pleasantly over them. What a pity that the one stone was missing from the middle of No. 7's door. All the others seemed entire. He glanced down the row. How could one fill it up? He looked again and something so simple, so easy and so obvious suddenly struck him that he hit his head with his fist as though it were made of wood.

It was his stone face which had come from there! Of course! The wedge-shaped base of stone on which it was carved was exactly that shape, it would fit exactly. Then it would stand there, in the middle of the archway, smiling with all its strength and confidence; then the whole face of No. 7 would come fully alive again. No. 7 was the only house which had such a gap, the smooth little arches of the other houses had obviously never been broken. Somehow, somehow before Aunt Emmeline came he must after all get it back again and get some mortar, or whatever was needed. . . . But first things first. His mind now whirling again with renewed possibilities and projects, he started scraping away at the lower panels in a frenzy of energy.

And at the same time that the face of Songberd's Grove was so impressing itself upon him, no less than four other people were thinking of it too.

CHAPTER

16

In Emandalf Aunt Emmeline and Uncle Alfred were lingering over the remains of a late lunch (if you could call it lingering, that is, for to linger over a meal suggests enjoyment). Uncle Alfred had been sent back from work with a feverish cold and this had put everything out; in consequence his wife felt very peevish. She was the delicate one anyway, and she felt that Alfred had no right to have a cold; she had to open some more packets from her stores and even cook some potatoes; in her displeasure she looked around for something to be unpleasant about.

"I'm going to see this place of William's on Tuesday," she said, pursing her lips and sniffing as though at a bad smell. William was her brother, Mr. Singer, and Martin had often wondered how two people so totally different in looks, character, feelings and everything else could have possibly managed to grow up in the same family.

"Williub's place? Oh, yes." A temperature and a thick cold made poor Alfred slow of comprehension; he was thinking longingly of bed, hot-water bottles and steaming kettles of inhalant, but knew that such kindly things were unlikely to be his lot.

"How he could ever marry that woman!" Aunt Emmeline took up again the cry that she had repeated so often since her brother's marriage that it had almost become her signature tune. All the things that displeased and annoyed her in life, and these were many, she piled onto the shoulders of her inoffensive sister-in-law, making her out to be a monster, riddled with every sort of fault.

"Oh, I dodt doe." Secretly Alfred was very fond of Dora Singer; life had seemed much pleasanter when she and Martin were about, and now, he felt, her comfortable round face expressing concern, she would be the first to get him off to bed, make him some soup that was real and not out of a packet, plump up the pillows behind him, half draw the curtains and tiptoe away again. . . . But his own wife Emmeline had risen to her feet.

"A proper hovel of a place I expect it'll be too!" she said scornfully. "I was talking to someone who delivers round that part of London yesterday, and he said it's nothing but slums. Slums! My brother William in a place like that, why, it upsets me even to think of it! And what kind of friends can they have? I don't know what I should do if any of the neighbours got to hear. That smart woman, Mrs. Jupp, for instance, who has just moved in down the road. Well, I shan't let Dora be in any doubt as to what we feel about it, letting her family down like that!"

"It was Williub who found the place," suggested Alfred timidly, but his wife gave him a look of withering scorn. Looking round for something to punish him with for this remark, her eyes fell on the table.

"That was the last packet of soup," she said. "Not a thing left in the store cupboard! As you're not doing anything, Alfred, and have got the whole afternoon for a holiday, you might just go out and fetch me two or three more. You know how important it is for me to put my feet up after lunch. I really don't think I could carry on, what with all I've got to do, if I didn't."

Resignedly, feeling alternately as cold as though it were January and then so hot that he wondered if the climate of England had suddenly become tropical,

Alfred fidgeted with a scarf, pulling it on and off his neck as he alternately shivered and burnt, and prepared for the journey to the shop, his wife's words still beating round his head like a hailstorm.

". . . what's going to happen to that Martin of theirs, I should like to know, brought up in a place like that? What sort of friends is he likely to make? He's a difficult enough boy as it is. Do you know, Alfred . . ." Alfred was feeling for the elusive front door now which seemed to have grown big and woolly and was shrinking away from his fingers as though it were playing touch with him.

". . . do you know, that Mrs. Jupp's daughter—ever such a pretty, dainty little thing she is, too—goes to a dancing-class where they've actually got one pupil whose aunt has got a title? . . ."

Lord Simon Vigo sat in his office, but offices and Lord Simon did not go together. To his nervous subordinates it always seemed that if he should stretch his large and powerful frame, or bellow with impatience or enthusiasm, as he was frequently apt to do, if he blew his nose too loudly or sneezed, the walls would fall apart like those of a card-house, leaving him in the large and open-air space which his personality seemed to require.

The figure which Mr. Triplett had once clothed so

reverently was now, in its late sixties, as impressive as in the days he had first known it; the mind which it housed was also as energetic and explosive as it had ever been. Having ridden full tilt at everything that had claimed his attention all his life, Lord Simon now found himself trustee for some property in London belonging to his cousin, the young Duke of Sarrat, and turned the full force of his attention on that, like a torch beam.

London for Lord Simon in his youth had meant his regiment and the barracks in which they were quartered, his clubs, the theatres and the elegant houses to which he went for dances and dinners. Everything he saw then had been prosperous, flourishing and well-kept; between the two wars he had mostly been abroad, and now, for the first time, as trustee of the estate, he came face to face with the other side of London. For the first few weeks, like a commanding officer inspecting his troops, he walked up and down and in and out of all the streets, alleys and terraces which belonged to the estate, and if he could have shouted to all the shabby, dilapidated houses to pipeclay themselves instantly and spring to attention, he would have done so. Failing the ability to do this, he went back to his office and thought hard.

The first necessity seemed to be a bicycle. He did not care for using his feet as a means of transport, a car was too cumbersome for some of the narrow streets of the Sarrat Estate, and though a horse was his favourite means of getting about, and would in fact have been most convenient, he rejected this on the ground that none of his horses would have liked it. From where it had stood neglected for years in an outhouse of his country home he brought up a gaunt but serviceable old machine with racing handle bars and an unexpected turn of speed and was on it, pedalling up and down the streets at a terrifying rate, before any of his despairing servants had time to get at it and clean it. The next thing he decided that he wanted was a go-ahead architect.

Brooding on this problem one week-end and when he was exercising the dogs at home, he left them happily ratting in the hedge outside the church-yard, and turned into the village church, where many of his ancestors were buried, to think it out. He had always found churches good places for problems. There was only one other person there, a small excitable man who was examining the stone-work in one corner and who, the moment Lord Simon came in, turned round, pink and spluttering with rage, as one whose feelings were too much for him.

"To have let it go like this!" he said, fizzing away like a glass of salts. "A gem of a village church, all these exquisite marbles, and look!" He pointed to the

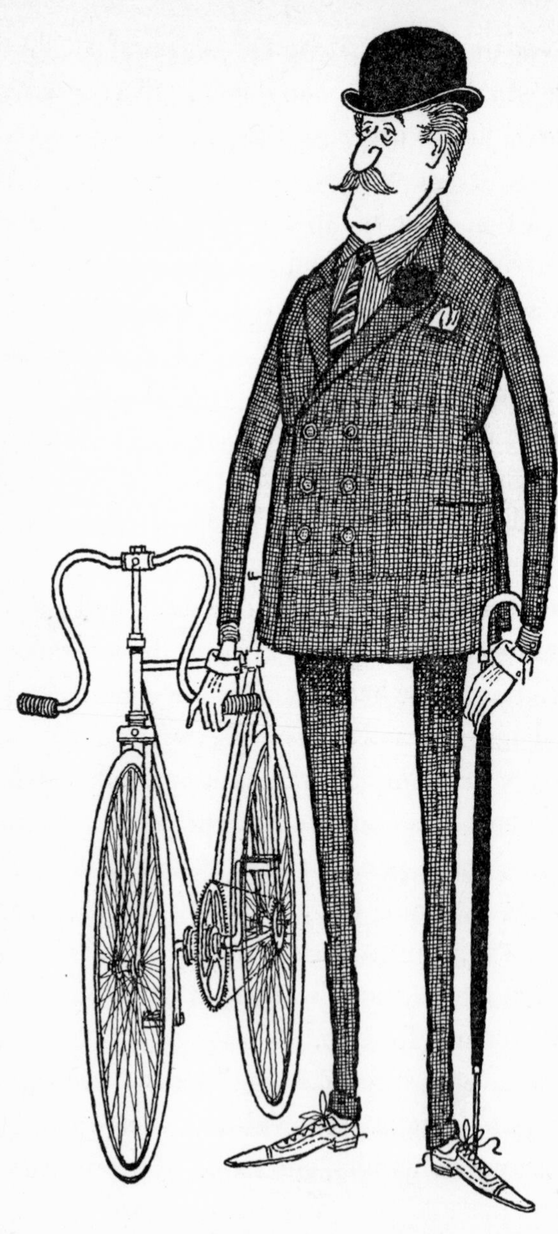

Lord Simon Vigo

low, rounded arch above his head and broke off a crumbling bit of stone, handing it indignantly to Lord Simon on his palm and unaware that he was talking to one of the Vigos, by whose effigies he was surrounded. "No cleaning, no restoration . . . they'll have it down round their heads before they know where they are!"

Lord Simon stared at the angry little man, stuck out his long legs from the pew and blew out his moustache. He liked people who felt strongly enough about things to get angry and he seemed to meet very few nowadays.

"You one of these architect fellows?" he asked.

"Yes." John Pim was still examining the stone with angry solicitude.

"Live near here?"

"No, in London."

"Where?"

"Prince Regent's Canal." The questions were delivered with such authority that John Pim found himself answering them automatically and without thinking, as though he were back in the army or at school.

"Good Lord! That runs through the Sarrat Estate. Like a job?"

This time John Pim did turn round and look at Lord Simon, and by the time they left the church, he found himself, slightly dazed but none the less delighted, consulting architect to the Sarrat Estate. He had also extracted a promise from his new employer to let him have the village church restored.

As time went on he found that he was considerably more than consulting architect; he was also blower-up of bicycle tyres and soother-down of office staff among a million other unexpected duties. But a brief and exciting war-time career in the army made him used to Lord Simon's ways, and their twin enthusiasms were already creating havoc among the age-old decrepitude of the Sarrat Estate. Distrusting bicycles as much as Lord Simon distrusted feet, he had bought himself the car in which Martin and Geneva had been given a lift, and now, with the car parked outside the office, he was standing in front of Lord Simon and fizzing as violently as on the first time that they had met in the church.

The way to deal with the Sarrat Estate, Lord Simon had long since decided, was exactly the same way as that in which he had always dealt with any body of men under his command. Pride. Give it pride. You couldn't expect any regiment to feel proud of itself in shabby uniforms and out-of-date equipment; all right then, how could the inhabitants of his estate take any pride in it if they lived in cracked and peeling houses with slummy streets in front of them? Systematically he was trying to get the whole area painted and tidied up, while the other trustees and the accountants wrung their hands in the background at the expense. But luckily, as the estate was a very rich one and Lord Simon's character extremely strong, in the background they remained.

As Lord Simon bicycled up and down and John Pim followed after him in his much less racy car, deciding which streets of the endless-seeming wilderness were to be tackled next, some interesting things came to light. Every now and again they came on a street of extreme architectural beauty, very old and hidden away behind dirt and grime; they had recently had one of these cleaned up and now people were to be seen down there all the time photographing and sketching it. Articles had been written about it in various reviews and Lord Simon was delighted with this first result of his campaign; it meant that the Sarrat Estate was beginning to be put on the map. If any such another street were found, he told John Pim, it was to be put instantly at the top of the cleaning list. And here was the little man hopping up and down in front of him now.

"I don't know what it's called," he said. "Either the name wasn't up or I didn't notice it—the circumstances were rather peculiar—but I could take you there. It's a gem, finer even than Barley Walk, but the strange thing is that it seems to me there's the touch of the same hand in both of them. I've been finding out quite a lot about the local eighteenth-century architects since we tidied that street up—there were two brothers who were responsible for all the best work and who were buried in the church they built. One seems to have been an architect and the other a sculptor and mason; they were great characters too, it seems, benefactors of all the local poor and needy, well loved and well thought of: Matthew and Nicholas——"

"All right, all right!" Lord Simon put up a hand to stop the flood of John Pim's enthusiasm. "It's a good street, is it? That's enough. We can go into flummeries like the names of the architects later, when we've got our work done." He glared at his consulting architect for a moment. "When can I see it?" He flicked over his engagement pad which seemed to bristle with the strokes of his impatient writing, ran his pencil down through them and eventually brought it to rest.

"Monday," he said. "Have to be evening. I'm busy all that day. Six-thirty. You can take me there in that contraption of yours. Well, I suppose we can finish now. I'm going down to the Albert Hall, heavyweights, y'know."

He sighed. "It's not what it used to be. Perhaps they don't eat enough meat nowadays, I don't know. But I wish some of the boys I used to watch in my youth were still here. Take Basher Byre now, the one that was killed at Dieppe. . . . What a waste!" He shook his head. "The most beautiful mover I ever saw. There was one special little step of his, shifted his weight in the fraction of a second like a dancer or a polo pony; nobody else ever seemed to get the hang of it, and now I don't suppose anybody ever will." Once again he shook his head.

"Monday evening, six-thirty sharp, then," he said.

Things were not going well for Lennie. Like the first touch of frost in the air which heralds the end of summer, he could feel something in the atmosphere of Songberd's Grove which seemed to be undermining his power, making him apprehensive and uncomfortable. All right, he'd show them! Glowering at the cupboard in which the head was hidden, that head which seemed to him to be the cause of all his bad luck, he went out into the row, determined to start up a new reign of terror and put things back in their place again. But somehow he seemed to have lost his touch.

The younger of the small fry, their heads filled now with all the intriguing and constructive ideas that Helga had been teaching them, were running about delightedly with the stick and paper lanterns which she had just shown them how to make and would pay no attention to him. Like a whole lot of flipping elves on a Christmas card! Lennie looked at them disgustedly and turned away to the larger ones. These were swarming together in a muttering group and one or two of the outside ones even dared to dart defiant looks at him. He picked up a stick and would have swished them one, only there was that yellow-haired doll sitting on a doorstep and looking at him with a soppy expression, and somehow . . . For once, had they known it, he and Geneva would have been in complete agreement.

Alan and Trevor were away, down at the market, and Rusty was nowadays a total loss.

Lost somewhere between babyhood, childhood and boyhood, none of which had ever had their due of affection, uncertain whether he wanted mother, sister, girl friend or all three, all Rusty's starved feelings, lit by the fire of his Irish temperament, had suddenly rushed out of him towards the beautiful and gentle Helga, and he had got it very badly indeed. A curious, delightful, yet at the same time painful and breathtaking feeling, somewhere between sea-sickness, pins-and-needles and extreme hunger, churned continually round inside him and, if he had been able to spell words of more than four letters, would surely have burst out of him in poetry. Even his mother, the most voluble of the talkers, noticed that he had gone off his food. As it was he did nothing but stand in front of No. 7 and stare, his blue eyes growing rounder and rounder every moment and as misty now as his native mountains. Giving him a sharp jab with his elbow as he passed, Lennie returned disgustedly to No. 1.

What was Songberd's Grove, anyway? Nothing but a beastly children's playground. He was getting too old for such things; of course, that's why he had this feeling—he had grown out of it. Dressing himself with special care he strolled out and away from it with haughty nonchalance and made his way towards the main street, where he joined up with his set of similarly dressed and similarly thinking youths. The strange uniform which they affected, the barrel-like jackets and the drain-pipe trousers, reduced the proportions of their bodies (which, being young and healthy, were presumably the same shape as everyone else's) to those of baboons; the sound of their laughter and the expression on their faces was equally ape-like. Lennie slipped in among them.

Most of them were older than he was and with more advanced ideas; at home he might be king of Songberd's Grove, but here he was small fry himself for a change. And, following on his general run of bad luck, the older ones were in a bad mood tonight, a mood in which they were just as ready to turn on one of their own band as on anyone else.

"You're slippin' a bit, aren't you, Len?" said one of them. "I went past that street of yours this morning and saw paint going up on doors and all sorts. Be having some fancy gardens and fountains out in front next, I suppose?" The others sniggered. Lennie was obviously going to be the bait today and they were ready to join in. The derelict state of Songberd's Grove, in which no milk bottle or tyre survived intact for longer than a day, his complete and destructive rule over it, had been Lennie's pride and boasting points to the boys. He coloured, put on his most scornful expression to hide his flush and laughed lightly.

"That's what you think," he said, "but I been doing some thinking, see? A bit more subtle than some of you chaps is capable of. Want to hear?" And knowing suddenly that he must either succeed now or sink and have to leave their ranks, he summoned his courage and stared down his nose at them as though he didn't care one way or the other what they thought.

For a moment it was touch and go, then his bluff worked. "Well, what is it, what you got up your sleeve?"

Lennie shrugged his shoulders.

"What's the fun in stopping people doing things the moment they've begun? There's no point in that. They get discouraged and give up and then where are you? Back where you started. No, the way I figured it out is this. . . ." Out of the side of his eye he was watching the boys anxiously, to see if the tide of their approval was still running with him. "Let 'em finish it, I say, paint up their doors and posh up their steps and everything and think they've got away with it; then, when they're all slapping each other on the back and sighing with relief and asking their friends round to admire, that's the moment to step in." He looked up again; things still seemed to be hanging in the balance.

"So I wondered if you boys would like a bit of sport on Monday?" he said lightly. "Saved it up for you like, in case you would. That's the day they reckon to be finished, I'm told." Mudface had, in fact, extracted this information from Rusty by various painful methods and passed it on to Lennie.

He had almost won.

"Sounds all right," said one of the older ones grudgingly. "Can't do any harm. It'll keep our hands in, anyway. What sort of time shall we meet?"

"Oh—sixish?" suggested Lennie, more lightly than

ever, and now unable to hide his relief. "Most of the parents are back from work and eating then. See you on Monday then."

As amateur in this as in all their other games, all talking at once and getting nowhere, the larger of the small fry were still in the middle of their indignation meeting when, like farmers bringing the cattle home at night, their mothers started calling to them from the various doorways. Reluctantly they started to move, feeling that much more was still to be said, but at least from the babble of excited small voices, which had been like an orchestra of squeaky violins tuning up, two definite things had emerged. They thought that Lennie had their football, their special and glorious football, hidden away in his room: they were going to get it back. The two oldest and most articulate lingered a little behind the others to restate their decisions.

"We'll watch 'im," said one, and the other nodded.

"When 'e goes out," went on the first one, "we'll all go in." At this gem of reasoning and strategy they looked at each other, nodded their heads sagely and suddenly broke into runs as their mothers' voices became slapping-shrill.

Outside the theatre, on her way home, La Golondrina paused to do up a shoe. It was now one of the most difficult things in life for her to do. Down, down went the creaking flesh and round it her small hands fumbled for the foot which they could only just reach and which she could no longer see. As she straightened herself again, having somehow done up the lace, she leant back against the wall for a moment with her eyes shut, to get back her breath.

It was covered in posters announcing next week's programme. As La Golondrina opened her eyes again the first thing she saw was a photograph that she had been leaning against, that of a dark, Spanish face. With her hand to her heart she took a quick step away.

Enrico Ribera! He was coming here! It seemed as though the pavement and the street were dissolving all round her, as though there were mountains and sun and the sound of guitars. It seemed as though she, La Golondrina, light as a feather, were just stepping out to face him, her childhood's sweetheart and partner. Mixing past and present in a blur she looked down to see if her shoes were well and truly fastened for the dance.

And could not see them, but only the mountainous body in between.

For almost the first time since she had been in England, La Golondrina realised fully what had happened to her. He would never dance with her again, perhaps would never even recognise her; it would be better if he did not. For a moment she beat her fists in anguish against his face on the poster, then slowly, as though she had aged twenty years in that minute, walked away.

The grey street seemed to stretch endlessly in front of her and just as endlessly life in Songberd's Grove, with no hope ever of any return to Spain. But there was suddenly a break in the greyness, a burst of light, a clatter of knives and conversation, an exquisite smell of frying fish.

Breaking her age-long rule, for she deeply distrusted any food not cooked and bought by herself, La Golondrina went in. To blot out the memory of that face she ordered a glass of wine and plate after plate of shellfish.

It was after the last one that she began to feel extremely ill, iller and iller, until the whole room spun round her and she knew that she could not get home. Gazing wildly round before everything blurred, she saw at one of the other tables the doorman from the theatre where she worked.

"Please, a taxi!" she gasped, and as he helped her into one, her muddled and whirling thoughts at last gave way. "Enrico Ribera," she whispered. "You tell him La Golondrina . . . No. 7 Songberd's Grove . . ." and she collapsed back on the seat of the taxi.

"That's the address, chum," said the doorman to the taxi driver, scratching his head. "Beats me what the rest of it is all about," and went away with the curious names still echoing through his mind.

CHAPTER 17

THE NEW paint on the door was really a tremendous success; sleepy and tired though he was, Martin could still appreciate it. Buying a tin at random, Mr. Singer had been lucky enough to strike a good one, and the shining depths of colour seemed to hold reflections of all the most gloriously red things in life: fire-engines and buses and traffic lights, geraniums and apples and bandsmen's uniforms. It somehow suggested trumpets to Martin, fires in winter and holly; it would look wonderful in the snow, he thought, running on a month or two. "If it's still there," he added to himself gloomily, for there was an absence of any sort of action on the part of Lennie and company which seemed to him most sinister and suspicious.

As though the door were the focal point of its existence, its mouth and its meaning of communication with the rest of the world, the house had fallen in place all round it and now looked infinitely better; only the gap in the archway seemed to cry out more than ever to be filled. Had it been given any say in the matter, his stone face, Martin felt sure, with a tug at his heart, would have chosen and approved of that red.

Beside it and complementing it perfectly the pale yellow door of No. 6 was now reinstated in its former glory. All through the weary Sunday afternoon, when Martin and Geneva had been on guard, groups of inhabitants from all down the row had come to admire, and the wives, suddenly becoming home- and street-conscious, had set on their husbands and demanded that their doors be painted too, argument rising high over the proposed colours.

"Green!" cried Rusty's mother. "Green for Old Ireland!" And her husband was despatched to buy brushes and a tin of paint forthwith. "Duck-egg!" "Orange!" "Black!" All the rest had their own ideas. If only all this had happened a week or two earlier, thought Martin bitterly, for whatever they did next week his main problem was still to keep Aunt Emmeline from seeing the rest of the row on Tuesday. He thought longingly of blinkers which could be clapped on as soon as she arrived.

The only exception to the general excitement and admiration was Lennie's mother, in No. 1. The colour of doors meant nothing to her, for she could see no beauty in the world other than Lennie's, and at the moment Lennie's behaviour was upsetting her considerably. Not only was it strangely distracted, absent-minded and mild, so that she longed for a shout, a complaint or a rough command from him as one might hope for a sick dog to bark as a sign of returning health, but there was something else about it which was worrying her to death. He was behaving exactly as his father used to behave before a big fight, and for the first time in many years she had been driven to think of Basher. Seeing Lennie almost fully grown and in the same mood as his father, it suddenly dawned on her dim perceptions that Lennie had become the spitting image of the Basher, and panic rose up in her. Ought she to move again? Plucking at her apron she moved distractedly about their rooms, burning Lennie's toast and ruining his coffee in her agitation, but never, to her ever-increasing dismay, getting any complaint from him.

The silence which seemed to her so frightening seemed to Martin merely ominous. From his pitch in front of Nos. 6 and 7, he discussed it with Geneva. During the last two nights he had camped out behind the bushes, as he said he would, slipping out through the garden gate and round after his parents had gone to sleep, and draping himself in a brown army blanket which acted as both protection and camouflage. Geneva had stationed herself at the window above and they had both uncomfortably dozed and nodded through the nights, rising jaded, stale and irritable.

Conditions all through the house, in fact, were in a state of extreme tension. La Golondrina was ill and Mrs. Singer had reached the furthest limits of nervous distraction; only Helga and her kindly parents, placid as beautiful cattle grazing peacefully through a thunderstorm, remained unmoved.

Sunday afternoon presented no difficulties because people were always about in the row then, and Martin and Geneva thankfully snatched some sleep. Monday was the problem, and, when it came, with a sudden stroke of inspiration, Martin got out an easel and canvas which his parents had given him for Christmas, took the kitchen stool and his paintbox and set up the whole apparatus outside the houses so that he had a slantwise view of No. 6 and No. 7, which he proceeded to sketch. But Martin's talent was for lettering and not for sketching; and by the time he had put the two doors in wrong and half washed them out again, getting them somehow mixed up with the sky in the process, the whole thing had taken on a very surrealist appearance.

As Geneva took over from him from time to time when he went indoors for meals, and, as she had ideas about colour as vivid as her ideas about food and life generally, their sketches grew more and more like a mad patchwork quilt. For like Penelope, wife of Ulysses, who undid her work every evening so that it should never be finished, every now and then they surreptitiously changed the sheet of paper and began all over again. In this present, the fourth version, Geneva, bored with the house front, was splashing in a glorified vision of La Golondrina at the window, a shawl hanging out over the sill beside her. Looking at it as he came back from strolling the length of the row to see if there were any enemy movement, Martin raised his eyebrows.

"Well, yours was so grey!" said Geneva explosively and defensively. "Everything in this country is grey. Look!" And she pushed the paint-box under his nose, pointing out the deep holes worn since this morning in the cakes of sepia, brown and black. She was now trying to work her way through some of the other colours and absent-mindedly, in her concentration on the shawl, took a great suck of what was on the brush.

"There's no pleasing you," said Martin mildly.

"One day it's yellow you don't like and now it's grey." He realised that the remark had been unfortunate as soon as he said it, for she darted him a look of fury before making a frightful face.

"Ugh! That tasted horrible! Martin! You don't think it's poison?" She rinsed her mouth with the drinking water they had brought and looked at him with round eyes before she went on.

"My mother has been poisoned, you know. It was some shellfish she ate, in a restaurant. The doctor says she is better now, but she cannot eat." She sighed profoundly. "The way everything always happens at once. There was a Spanish dancer, a man, coming to the theatre, that she used to dance with once. He would have surely recognised her—for she is in hiding here, you know," Geneva raised her head proudly. "Incognito—pretending not to be La Golondrina until my education is finished; only she cannot keep away from the theatre. He would probably have insisted that she go back instantly to Spain and dance, whether I am educated or not!"

Fully believing this wild version of the facts, for one moment Geneva made her mother and herself sound like princesses of blood royal, their actions and the state of their education vital to the future of Europe.

Then, with one of her lightning changes she

slumped down into gloom again. "But what is the use? It will be weeks, I think, before she goes back to the theatre. He will come, and be gone. . . . I left a message for him when I went to tell them she was ill, but will they deliver it?" She made a gesture with her hands and then started wildly splashing black into the middle of the shawl to match her thoughts. "She will not eat . . . I make omelettes, I cook rice . . . all, all in the dust-bin."

Martin looked at her with concern. It seemed that parents were always a problem and an anxiety. He too had seen La Golondrina. It was as though the tide of flesh which had flowed over her for so long had suddenly turned and was slipping the other way, stripping her of all her years of accumulated fat. But, because she looked so ill and was so listless, because she no longer had the heart to dye her hair and it was black again and dull with ill-health, like seaweed taken out of water, neither he nor Geneva realised that the grace had come back again to her few and feeble gestures. Before, her movements had been those of someone moving limbs beneath the muffling folds of a cloak, now they had in them once again the rhythm of all the music on which she had been nourished, the arabesques of the swallows across the mouth of that far-off cave.

Sucking in her lower lip after the paint, Geneva

shook her head and looked down the row. "What are they doing?"

Martin had been pursuing his own thoughts. "It's a quarter to six already. It's an extraordinary thing, but Lennie's gone out. If only we can hold them off tonight . . ." And then he realised that Geneva had said something. "Who?"

"Them." She gestured towards the small fry, who were behaving in a most extraordinary manner. As though they were a collection of dust particles blown together into a ball by the wind, they would converge on one another and start advancing towards the far end of the row together, then, at any noise or sudden fright, as though the same wind had suddenly veered and blown them apart, they would scatter and run back again. They evidently were trying very hard to steel themselves to do something, and suddenly, all at once, they dashed in through the door of No. 1.

Martin shrugged his shoulders. "One of their daft games, I expect," he said, and looked round for Helga, who was usually with them nowadays.

Made perceptive by jealousy, Geneva interpreted his glance. "She's gone out too—she went past while you were watching Lennie. So did the Bolsoms."

Martin looked at her and a goose-shiver ran down his spine. Somehow, although everything looked so innocent and so peaceful, in a way which he couldn't explain, he felt as though a stage were being set for something, with all unnecessary actors removed; as though decks were being cleared for action. Even the cleaning-women had gone off to the local cinema. The evening, too, was growing every minute more hushed and apprehensive, as if waiting for something; the hot sky was still and brassy and there was thunder about somewhere. Even the roar of the distant traffic seemed to be muffled.

As though two more characters had yet to walk off, the splendid door of No. 7 opened and his own parents came out. For a moment Mr. Singer looked at his handiwork with justifiable pride, touched it lightly with one finger and looked rather patronisingly across to Mr. Bolsom's blaze of yellow, pointing out to his wife a bit of imperfect brushwork on the latter. Mrs. Singer looked, nodded dutifully, and fell back into her inner preoccupations. The nervous strain of waiting for tomorrow's visit was making her feel every bit as ill as Uncle Alfred with his cold, and she was a shadow of her usual self.

"Taking your mother to the pictures," said Mr. Singer, looking doubtfully over Geneva's shoulder at the extraordinary daub on the easel. They've got Ted Chanteclere playing his trumpet at the Phillipo." For as everyone has one relief to which they turn in time of trouble, whether it be aspirin, a hot bath or a cup of tea, Mr. Singer, who was very worried about his wife, considered trumpet music to be the most soothing and unfailing balm that he knew.

He pointed to the extraordinary shawl in the picture. "Sure you still want that thing sticking out of the window?" And as Martin nodded: "So long, see you about nine, then." And Mr. and Mrs. Singer set off down the Grove, Martin's eyes following them. Just what would they see at nine? Somehow, one way or another, he knew that the issue would be settled by then.

Except for the wraith of La Golondrina upstairs and the bee-like humming of Mr. Triplett's sewing-machine from the back, he and Geneva were alone now in front of the two houses. He called on his inner man for strength and to make sure that he was in touch.

It was not a moment too soon. Round the far corner of the row, the moment that his parents had disappeared, swaggering jauntily, and as cat-like as his father had been, came the figure of Lennie.

After a fraction of a moment of silence Geneva caught Martin's arm.

"There's more of them!" she exclaimed in a horrified whisper. "He's brought people from outside!" For, as well as Trevor and Mudface, who joined the party as it came in, like a troop of black-clad ants, baboons or Martians, all the thin-legged, T-shouldered Teddy boys of the district were crowding in behind Lennie. As they advanced down the row, scattering the small fry, who were out again like a drift of dusty leaves, Martin and Geneva rose to their feet behind the easel and backed towards the doors.

"This all you brought us to?" sneered the largest Martian. "Couple of kids playing with paints? Hardly worth our while." As he turned to Lennie and made as if to walk away it gave Martin and Geneva a moment to get themselves organised.

The plan had been for them to defend one door each, but now, with the enormous number of their opponents, this seemed to Martin impossible. He took a swift decision. The defences of the red door were better organised; the yellow door must go.

"Back to No. 7!" he said quickly to Geneva. "We'll both guard that." But he had reckoned without Geneva.

"There are two doors," she said, her eyes flashing, "and they shan't get either! Eight of them, the cowards, they'll see!" Seizing the long-legged easel as a weapon she fled back and flattened herself against the door of No. 6, her black hair vivid against the yellow paint. As Lennie still argued and pleaded with the boys, Martin made a flying dash inside No. 7, turned on the sink tap, reached for something through the window and was back with the door shut behind him and something in each hand.

As the boys still wavered he let the leader have the contents of one in the face to make up their minds for them. Attack was the best form of defence. One way or another he wanted this thing settled, now, once and for all. If by some miracle he and Geneva could keep them off until some grown-ups appeared . . .

As the bag of flour burst on the astonished Martian, he gave a yell of fury and disgust and ran forward, brushing it out of his eyes. Martin took his thumb off the nozzle of his hose he held in his other hand, which led out through the window from the sink, and let him have that full blast, turning the flour to a sticky mash and drowning his shout as the water splashed into his mouth.

It was a momentary advantage but it could not last for long. For Lennie too this was something which had to be settled here and now. His whole position and way of life was at stake. Forgetting his junior position among the Teddy boys, he called up Trevor and Mudface and took charge of the proceedings, dividing them with a gesture and setting one lot on each door. Startled at his cheek but swept away by his authority, the others obeyed, Trevor and his men rushing Geneva, while the others, their hands and their pockets full of stones, advanced slowly but menacingly upon Martin.

With wild shouts Geneva laid about her with the easel, flailing it in a flying arc in front of her so that no one could come nearer to her than the bottom step, while Martin, silent and white with determination, directed the hose on the faces of his furious opponents. Had Geneva kept up her flailing movement all might have been well, but the triumph had gone to her head and she wanted something more spectacular. Seeing Trevor's hated flap of pale hair in front of her she raised the easel above her head to bring it down on him, and in that moment was undone. Two of the others got in under her defences and rushed forward to kick at the door while Trevor, catching hold of an easel leg pulled it from her grasp. Defenceless except for teeth, nails and feet and ready to use them all, Geneva stood panting and breathless and with flashing eyes, spreadeagled against the door, as though she were the sole defender of some mediæval fortress. Almost in admiration the boys in front of her paused for the fraction of a second, and then surged past her once more, kicking at the yellow paint and scraping it with stones, trying to pluck her away from where she clung kicking and biting, one hand on the door handle and the other on the knocker.

Seeing her predicament Martin straddled himself sideways across the approach to his own door and trained the hose on her opponents. For a moment it halted them so that he could see Geneva raise her head and look with wild hope towards someone who had just bicycled into Songberd's Grove. Then, as he strained to get Trevor in its range there was a sudden sickening squelch and the thing went limp and waterless in his hands. It had pulled away from the tap. Looking desperately at Martin as the water ceased, realising the situation, Geneva suddenly put her head down and wriggled through the crowd in front of her, who were too much interested in trying to reach the door to stop her flight. Martin just had time to see her leap onto a strange bicycle and ride madly away before his own position claimed his full attention. Good old Geneva, who could blame her for panicking now? Not many would have stayed there for as long as she had.

While the hose was no longer on them and Martin's attention had strayed, Lennie and the others had advanced to within striking distance of the door. The first stone touched it. As though it were his own skin which had been cut Martin suddenly went into a wild and berserk fury, seizing with both hands the small bags of flour which he had spent every spare minute preparing and stacked in two buckets beside the red door, banging them down on each face as it rose in front of him and kicking out at the same time, trying to get at knees, shins or anywhere he could reach. Lennie's rage was not concentrated on the door any longer but on Martin; here was the possible new leader of the street, here was the thing that must be destroyed. He rushed forward to try to seize Martin's hands, and as he came another heavy stone grated on the door.

Once again the wound on the paint was like a sharp physical pain to Martin. He suddenly reached with one hand behind him, turned the handle and sent the door flying inwards. Fool that he was to have its precious surface a flat and easy target behind him! Open, it was far more difficult to reach, only now he had to guard the gap to stop them coming into the hall. If only Mr. Triplett would hear, if someone would come, anyone, anyone! He groped for more flour and flung it straight into the face of a newcomer.

The bicycle on which Geneva had fled belonged to a telegraph boy. He had come with a telegram for No. 7 and had propped his machine up against the hedge while he looked for the number, asking Rusty, who was hanging about uncertainly on the fringes of the fray. There seemed to be some sort of scrum going on outside the house he wanted; but he was a telegraph boy of character; he had a telegram to deliver and did not intend to be put off. Teddy boys too, as he now recognised them to be from their strange, though no longer natty, contours, were his natural enemies, and he was never loath to take a crack at them. Lastly, being British, and seeing one chap fighting alone, he was instantly on that chap's side.

" 'Ere, chum," he said, shaking the flour from his face. And having scrambled up the steps and pushed the telegram through the letter-box, for it was obviously no good to ring, he squared his shoulders and stood with his fists ready in the gap beside Martin. The ammunition of flour being at last exhausted, the two of them proceeded to fight for the door as desperately as the defenders of Thermopylae.

At that moment there were only four boys against them and because of the narrowness of the doorway they could just manage to hold them off. But suddenly, the once-yellow door of No. 6 being now down to the bare wood again and offering no further pickings, the four boys from next door surged across to join them and by sheer weight started forcing their way inwards. At that moment something else happened too.

His finger in his mouth and in an agony of indecision, Rusty had been watching the fight. He didn't want to join Lennie and he had received no orders; the fate of the doors meant nothing to him, for his thoughts were above them, on the first floor. He did not know that Helga had gone out and kept hoping, as he always did nowadays, that she might look out. After the telegraph boy had asked him the number he had watched his progress to the door, then, to his horror, he had seen the dreadful thing.

The door, the door leading up to Helga's flat, was open! With sticks, stones and knives now the crowd of boys were fighting their way into No. 7, and Helga, all unprotected, was above.

With a wild, inarticulate cry he ran forward and somehow, driven by his singleness of purpose, and using very much the same methods as Geneva, he bit, kicked and scratched a way for his small body through the fighters, reaching the steps and turning so quickly that he tripped Lennie up, blocking the others and stemming, just in the nick of time, the forward rush into No. 7.

By the time Lennie, mad with rage, had picked himself up, the three of them, Rusty, Martin and the telegraph boy had formed themselves into a wedge in the doorway. In the brief lull Martin and the telegraph boy had pulled the heavy hat-stand round as a block behind them, armed themselves with the sticks and umbrellas it contained and now stood three deep in front of it, each striking out at his own level.

While a hail of stones crashed all round them the lanky telegraph boy struck at heads, Martin at chests and Rusty, now uttering strange cries and with his eyes glittering, whanged away at all the knees and feet within reach.

For a while they held out. Martin, a trickle of blood running down one cheek from where a stone had caught him, and in terror every minute for his glasses, swished about in front of him like a demon and shouted encouragement to the other two, but he knew it was only a question of time. The telegraph boy, his hat round the back of his neck and his face still clown-like with flour, responded enthusiastically, but he had arrived short of breath from his bicycling and was getting shorter every minute. Rusty gave a sudden cry and clapped his hand over his face as a knobby knee struck it. Then he was fighting back again, in spite of a black and swelling eye, but now with only the cracked stump of a broken umbrella.

"If only we can hold out a little longer!" thought Martin. "If only somebody would come!"

Realising that new tactics were needed, Lennie had paused for a moment and motioned the boys backward, gathering them for a new running charge up the steps. Looking desperately along the row as he braced himself for this, hoping against hope that someone might appear, Martin could hardly believe his eyes when he actually did see something come whizzing in at the far corner. It was a bicycle! The telegraph boy's bicycle with two figures on it! In front, pedalling wildly, was the stocky figure of John Pollard, and behind on the step, her black hair loose in the wind, was Geneva. They came flying over the pot-holes in the row, threw down the bicycle and charged the rear of the crowd. Almost hysterical with relief, Martin shouted and waved his stick in the air.

Hearing the sound and surprised in mid-charge, Lennie's boys wavered, half-turned and found themselves being set upon by what seemed to be a wildcat and a bear. As unnerved by Geneva's shrill cries as they were by John Pollard's bulk, they hesitated in their forward rush, turned to find out what was happening and saw something that threw them into final confusion.

Round the near corner of the row came a car. It swerved to a standstill and decanted two people. As the first one, a small, thin and excited man, came out they did not move, but as the magnificent, upright figure of the second emerged, old though he evidently was, a tremor of doubt ran through them. They looked first at him and then at each other and then, like birds suddenly leaving a field altogether without any apparent signal, Trevor and Mudface with them, they were gone. The moment they saw Lord Simon they had recognised it, the only thing in life that they feared and the only thing that they respected—the unmistakable, rarely met aura of true authority.

Catching a whiff of it in his turn, the telegraph boy suddenly remembered who he was and what he was supposed to be doing, clapped his hat back on his head, ran for his bicycle and disappeared out of sight. Only as he was several streets away and nearing his post-office again did he begin to wonder what the fight had been all about.

Like a bull who has escaped from his fellow cattle and stands bewildered in a deserted market-place, Lennie stood alone in the front of No. 7. Like a bull's, too, his thoughts were red. His world had come crashing round his ears. He knew he was finished with the boys now, and he had lost the leadership of the Grove. He was down, and as though to add to the bitterness a cloud of small fry suddenly came whining and squeaking all round him like a crowd of gnats, pointing to something they had brought with them wrapped up in a cloth, complaining about something, demanding something. The little so-and-so's! He'd show them if he was finished, if they could treat him like this! He'd show everyone!

The mêlée by the doorstep had brought out some strange instinct in his blood; for the first time in his life he wanted someone to fight and measure himself against—the largest, toughest thing that he could find. Seeing the tall, broad figure of Lord Simon through a blur of rage and oblivious of his age, he lunged and hit out with his fist.

Surprised, but with a movement that was almost second nature to him, Lord Simon side-stepped and parried the inexpert blow, sending Lennie tottering back with his weight on the wrong foot and nearly tripping over one of the small fry. At his failure the rage inside him seemed to burst. Somewhere, from way back inside Lennie, his feet and his hands remembered something that they had once been taught to do. Without any instructions from him they performed a quick little shifting dance on their own and were going forward again, all the weight of his body behind his fist this time. It made contact and a singing sense of achievement ran through his veins.

It did not last long. The mists cleared and he found himself standing and looking down at an elderly man who was now sitting on the steps—the rest of the crowd twittering round him—and feeling his jaw. Lost the boys and lost the Grove; gone and bashed an old chap now who'd call the cops for sure. This was the end. As there was nothing else to do, Lennie sucked his knuckles and waited.

The old boy looked up. Got to hand it to him, it didn't seem to have shaken him up much. He had a sort of dazed look in his eyes as if he couldn't quite believe what he had seen. Might be concussed, thought Lennie. At the thought of it he came out in a cold sweat.

"What's your name, boy?"

He could speak then, that was something. That's right, usual stuff, he was going to tell the cops.

"Lennie Byre."

"It *is*?" Lennie began to think that it was he who had been concussed, for the old boy rose to his great height and looked down at him incredulously.

"Your name is Byre? The son of Basher Byre? I knew it! There's no one else who could have taught you that. You're the spitting image of him too, now that I come to look at you. Basher's son!"

What in the world was he talking about? "Dunno what my father was," mumbled Lennie sulkily. It wasn't true, of course, but he wasn't going to say, not with all these people, Martin in particular, round him listening.

"You don't know?" The old man was incredulous

again. "They never told you? My boy," he said simply, "your father was the best heavy-weight boxer I ever saw." He turned to John Pim.

"We could do with a son of Basher's at the club, couldn't we, Pim? Haven't got many heavy-weights. I don't know if there's still time to teach you . . ." He considered Lennie appraisingly and handed him a bit of paper with an address. "Better come along and see me anyway."

But Lennie, taking the paper almost without noticing it, was still grappling with one idea.

"Heavy-weight? You mean a boxer?" he said. "Then he wasn't anything to do with flowers, then?"

"Flowers!" Lord Simon had to sit down again to laugh.

After a while he recovered himself, wiping his eyes. "Well, what's this all about?" he said, and looked round.

On the step above him, panting, dishevelled but triumphant, sat a nice-looking, red-haired boy, evidently the leader of one side of the operations, who grinned as he caught Lord Simon's eye and then scrambled to his feet. A small chap, with one bright blue eye and the other closed and black, stood panda-like beside him, still enthusiastically going over the motions of the fight with his hands, as though he were wound up and couldn't stop. Pollard and Pim and a black-haired girl were gesticulating together out in front of the houses, and a crowd of very small urchins, carrying something which seemed to be very heavy between them in a cloth, kept milling about like a shoal of minnows, looking for somewhere to put it down.

"You see, sir?" Brushing aside the human dramas that were being played out all round him, as though they were keeping everyone from the real purpose and excitement of the visit, John Pim felt anxiety only for the houses, and he kept rushing forward with little tender and clucking noises to feel the walls.

". . . those archways, those fanlights, the unmistakable hand of a master . . . ah!" For Martin had pushed the stand back once more and the half-open red door showed behind him again, with the long window behind it in the hall.

"What a perfect picture!" cried John Pim and looked up to the gap in the arch above it. "If only we still had the original corbel stone! A head it would have been, a goddess, or a satyr . . . but still, sir, as you see, the whole row is exquisite, well worth restoring, even without it. . . ."

The small fry, tearful and exhausted now and desperate to know what to do with their burden, looking around for help and recognising Martin as the new figure of authority in the row, suddenly staggered up the steps and dumped the cloth they were holding at his feet. It fell open, and the stone head lay smiling serenely at all of them.

CHAPTER

18

For a moment everyone stared at it, then, in the same second, both Martin and John Pim moved forward. His face! Martin wanted to snatch it up and run with it through into the privacy of his own room; but the necessity of hiding his feelings in front of all these people stopped him. And in any case John Pim had beaten him to it; he was down on his knees in front of it already, muttering to himself.

"Perfect! Beautiful! The most extraordinary likeness to something . . ." he said, puzzled. "These heads weren't usually portraits, of course, but every now and then, stands to reason, a man couldn't resist copying the features of some fellow mason. But it's so extraordinarily like an engraving or a picture I've just seen—now who . . ." His questing fingers had reached the base and he was feeling the initials.

"N.S. and M.S. Why two lots?" He looked up, frowning, and suddenly his eyes widened.

"What did you say the name of this row was?" he almost shouted.

"Songberd's Grove." It seemed to Martin, itching to get the head back to himself again, that the poor chap had gone completely batty.

"But of course! This must have been where they actually lived then. That's whose portrait it is! Those two brothers, Lord Simon, the ones that I told you about, the one an architect and the other a sculptor. Matthew and Nicholas Songberd! Oh, this is the most wonderful discovery. This will put the Sarrat Estate on the map all right!"

"Which was which?" Geneva had come up beside Martin and they looked down at the face.

"Which? Oh, Nicholas was the architect and Matthew the sculptor. This would be Nicholas."

"Nicholas Songberd!" They said his name over softly as they looked down at their friend.

"Of course he fits here, in this gap in the arch. A sort of signature to the house, you might say. Well, what do you say, sir? Can we begin the restorations here right away?"

"What's that, Pim? What's that?" In spite of his vigour Lord Simon was not as young as he had been, and his head was reeling from the events of the last half hour. Arrived here in the middle of some sort of rugger scrum and then been dotted one by a youth who turned out to be old Basher's son, had a stone head roll out of a cloth in front of him like something out of the French Revolution, and then Pim going off into long ecstasies and rambling on about songbirds. To add to his confusion someone was darting about behind him like a lunatic, exclaiming and brushing the dust off his shoulders.

"That's enough now, stop it!" he said testily and half-turned to see who his tormentor was. A distressed pink and white face peering over gold-rimmed half-spectacles, came up under his arm.

"Good lord! Old Tom Triplett from Cantrell's! And what in the name of heaven are you doing here?"

"I live here, my lord. Oh, you must let me take you in for a moment and let me put a stitch where you've split the seam. Oh, my lord, I can hardly believe it—it's one of my own coats still, one that I made you fifteen years ago!" The old man's voice was trembling with pride and emotion.

"Of course it is. You don't suppose I can find work like yours anywhere nowadays, do you? I've still got 'em all; though, come to think of it, I'm due for a few more. Tom Triplett here, who'd believe it! Well, as we've come on business we'd better look at these houses of yours, Pim. I've another engagement at eight."

Accompanied by John Pollard, they moved off down Songberd's Grove, and as though a fire had been kicked out and scattered into sparks, various dying fragments of the battle seemed to flare up for a moment and then go out. As Martin and Geneva watched from the doorway they saw Helga come in, catch sight of Rusty's eye and run forward in consternation to examine it. Martin grinned as he heard Geneva's disgusted exclamation and saw Rusty's other eye rolling in unbelievable bliss. Mothers came out and led away small fry to be bathed; only one of the larger ones remained, bitterly weeping.

Because his own mood was now despondent Martin had a fellow feeling for him; a queer and heavy sensation of responsibility, the loneliness of leadership, seemed to have settled on him too. He walked over and put a hand on his shoulder. "What's the matter, old chap?"

Between the gulps and sobs, it was difficult to understand.

" 'E took our ball, 'e did, and 'id it!" A grimy small hand wiped a grimy small face frantically and then jerked down to where Lennie, still looking at the address on the bit of paper Lord Simon had given him, had disappeared dazedly into No. 1. " 'E turned it into stone!" And on a wild and wailing crescendo at the thought of such sorcery, he started off again.

"Your ball?" Martin stared at him for a moment and then went into the hall. "This it?" he said, and he tossed out the one he had retrieved from the garden.

Catching at the precious object, round-eyed through his tears and fearful of losing it once more, the urchin rushed indoors. Alone and tired and despondent and suddenly finding themselves exhausted, Martin and Geneva went back to sit on the doorstep, the litter of the battle all round them and all the excitement over. A great gloom descended on them.

"So that's that," said Geneva, and they needed no further words to express their thoughts.

Lennie was beaten. Lord Simon might be giving his approval to the restoration of the row and ultimately it might be better, but that was in the future and they could not imagine it now. All that Martin could think of was the mess among which they sat, the fact that his parents would be coming back any minute now, and that the Visit was for tomorrow. He knew he had no longer even the energy to clear up the flour from the steps. Geneva's thoughts were further away, with the dancer who should have seen and recognised her mother, and who now never would, about whom her mother had been lamenting endlessly all day. At a call from the window above them she dragged herself wearily to her feet and made to go indoors.

Another, surprising noise from behind her made her turn—someone was saying something in Spanish! As she and Martin had looked at each other and then up as La Golondrina called, a little man in a black suit had come silently up to the front of the house without them noticing. He was short and stout, with curly grizzled hair and a curly-brimmed black hat held to his broad chest as though he were about to bow. In his kindly face his dark, spaniel eyes were full of anxiety.

"La Golondrina?" he asked, in a voice as round and rolling and foreign as his figure, as anxious as his eyes. "She live here, no? The doorman at the theatre 'as tell me . . ." and as he gestured with his other hand they saw that he was holding an immense sheaf of flowers, almost as big as himself.

"La Golondrina?" Suddenly, from beside Martin, Geneva burst into a torrent of Spanish, ran forward to the newcomer and took him by the arm, pointing upstairs and gesticulating wildly. His expression changed to one of delight, and an answering flood of words rushed out from him. Waving his hat and the flowers, flinging out first one arm and then the other, he followed Geneva into the house, a trail of scattered carnations strewing the steps and the hall behind him as they disappeared.

So now he was really alone; even the stone face had been taken away by John Pim. Martin braced himself for the one thing more that had to happen. Sure enough, before the sound of Geneva and her countryman had vanished up the stairs, he saw the figures of his father and mother turn in at the end of the row.

His father's remedy had worked; still with the celestial wafts of trumpet music ringing in their ears the two of them walked arm-in-arm towards Martin as though on clouds. He had to watch their faces slowly fall.

"What . . ." began Mrs. Singer, and then Martin's face, the trickle of dried blood where the stone had caught him, the state of his clothes and the steps made everything clear. She knew what he had been fighting for and she knew that he had lost, and instantly, at the sight of his silent misery, all her own worries fled from her as though they had never been, leaving nothing but a desire to comfort him. She stood for a moment in front of her flour and mud-spattered steps and the battered door and looked at him.

"Well, it's our home, isn't it? We like it, so what's the odds? What does it matter what anyone else thinks?" And suddenly, surprisingly, she found it was true. What did it matter? Feeling as light-hearted as though she had suddenly been given wings, in that moment she realised that she was freed from Aunt Emmeline's opinions forever.

One arm already through her husband's, she stuck the other through her son's, looked up at the house with new eyes and then, between her two men, started to rock helplessly with laughter.

"Coo, I can't half wait to see her face to-morrow, can you? 'Dora!' " Imitating her sister-in-law, she minced up the steps, and then went back to her own voice again.

"What's been going on here, I should like to know —a battle of flowers? Well, come on, let's have our supper. There's shrimps." And she opened the door of their house.

It was not until they closed the hall door behind them that they saw the telegram.

"Alfred got flu," it said when they opened it. "Unable come tomorrow. Emmeline."

CHAPTER

19

"Is THIS the right stop?"

"That's right, Mother; round by the church there and you can't miss the name." The conductor winked and made as if to help her down.

"I am perfectly well able to get off by myself, thank you!" Mother! Her lips pursed in fury, Aunt Emmeline got down. Mother, when even Mrs. Braby next door had complimented her on her new hat and said how smart she looked! Not that she wouldn't have every excuse in the world for looking more than her age at the moment, she thought, as she looked angrily after the departing bus, after all she had been through in the last few weeks. Men! And men when they were ill!

When Alfred's cold turned to flu and got nasty, the doctor seemed to think she had nothing better to do than to run about cooking and looking after him all day—and him knowing how delicate she was herself. Why, he had never said a word about it! And now, insult to injury, when Alfred was convalescent again and could have turned round and looked after her a bit, if his employers hadn't sent him off to the Isle of Wight! She was the one who needed a holiday, not Alfred, after all his pampering, but it was always the way. Men! They clung together. Well, she must have some consolation and take it out on somebody. Setting her hat on more firmly and clutching the string-bag without which she never went anywhere, she set off to visit her brother William and his wife.

Just the sort of district she had expected! Sniffing, with her nose in the air, Aunt Emmeline walked along the street the bus conductor had indicated, alert to criticise and condemn. She turned by the church and into the wide street off which lay Songberd's Grove. Slummy, as she had thought, children playing about in the street, paper in the gutters—a disgusting place for her brother to live! Like a war horse scenting battle, almost happy now at the thought of what she would be able to say to Dora, Aunt Emmeline went on.

Was this the one? She peered in towards the name over the row of houses; it said "Songberd's Grove." She had come in by the far end of the row, by No. 1 and was slightly upset to find that this had been newly painted. But still, what mean little houses and in what dingy surroundings, whatever sort of friends and neighbors could they have here! No. 7 must be at the other end of the row. Aunt Emmeline advanced.

All the houses had been painted, their stone-work cleaned, their window-panes mended, their front doors now shining in many colours of the rainbow, according to the owner's fancy, and a lorry-load of new gravel smoothed out over where the potholes had been in front of them. Increasingly ill at ease Aunt Emmeline went on and looked up at No. 7.

Ah, there was something going on there! Her spirits revived. A crowd of cars outside in the road and a mass of children in front of the house, people leaning out of the upper windows and someone shouting something through a megaphone. Even . . . yes, it was written on one of the cars, she thought she had seen it, "Press"! What could it be? Some sordid crime or other—what could you expect in this sort of district? She quickened her steps and found herself on the outskirts of the crowd.

"Nicholas Songberd," the voice through the megaphone was saying, "who lived, worked and died here in this house . . . discovered in the garden . . ." and the flashlight of a photographer flared. What was it, had he been murdered then; had someone dug him up? On tiptoe and agog Aunt Emmeline peered forward through the crowd, and at the top of the steps, in the very middle of the limelight, saw her brother and sister-in-law and their child.

But if it was a horrible crime which had been committed, they ought not to be looking like that! Dora, beaming with happiness, was laughing to William beside her, and that Martin, his glasses shining, was laughing too and shaking hands with the very tall old man who had been speaking. They paused for a moment as one more picture was taken, and then the party seemed to break up, some of the onlookers drifting away and the people who had been in the forefront going into the house. Pushing her way through the remaining fringe of people, Aunt Emmeline at last saw the full front of the house. It was as clean and well-painted as the rest of them, but it had two things that the others didn't have. One was a stone head stuck in the centre of the arch above the door; the other was a brand-new pale-blue plaque on the wall. She read the wording on the latter hastily. NICHOLAS SONGBERD, ARCHITECT, AND MATTHEW SONGBERD, SCULPTOR, LIVED HERE—and the dates; then she hurried through the door after all the retreating backs. As she did so the face over the door seemed to wink at her, much as that impertinent conductor had done. Gazing affrontedly back, she went in.

There was a clatter of tea-cups, of talk and of laughter; among it all, in the sunny room and completely at home, her sister-in-law went to and fro with the sugar and milk. So it was her room and her party. Aunt Emmeline pushed forward.

"Emmeline! Well, fancy you coming today, and such a to-do as we are having; I must find you a cup. This is Mr. Triplett, who lives next door to us. Mr. Triplett, this is my sister-in-law." And as though she, Emmeline, were of very little consequence, Dora Singer hurried away laughing as the tall old man said something to her. Emmeline turned to Mr. Triplett and saw to her extreme distaste that he had just dipped his ginger nut into his cup and was sucking with enjoyment its exquisitely soggy edge. Common! Of course, what could you expect? Finding her own level, that's what Dora was.

Her Own Level

The tall man came towards them, and Dora, returning with a cup, said: "Oh, Lord Simon . . . this is my sister-in-law, Mrs. . . . Emmeline, this is Lord Simon Vigo."

A lord! Emmeline was preparing some suitable remarks, but Lord Simon only gave her a brief bow and then turned to the old tailor. "Well, Tom," he said, "I can't get over finding you here, you know—by jove, that's the way to eat a ginger biscuit. Young Martin, d'you think you could go and find me one?" And as Martin departed, grinning, he turned to Aunt Emmeline.

"Your nephew, I suppose? He's a fine young chap." Turning back to Tom Triplett, he became absorbed in a conversation about the finer points of tailoring and paid no more attention to Aunt Emmeline.

Affronted once more, she moved back against the wall, from where people seemed to move perpetually past her. Occasionally as William or Dora passed, they found time to introduce her to one of them, "Mr. Pollard, who paints ever such lovely pictures, Emmeline; Mr. Pim . . ." Neither of these seemed to have time or inclination to spare for her intellectual conversation, and a fair, pleasant-looking woman, obviously the mother of a lovely girl who was with her, was next brought up.

"Mrs. Rosegg, from Switzerland . . ." Aunt Emmeline was by now absolutely determined to say something, to establish herself as a personality and to prove her worth.

"Switzerland—now isn't that where those lovely packet soups come from? Mrs. Rose Egg (what an extraordinary name!), we use them all the time." And she waited expectantly for Mrs. Rosegg's approval.

"Packets?" said the Swiss woman. "You make the soup from packets at your house?" She shook her head. "They are only for export—we would not have such stuff, eh, Friedrich?" Laughingly taking her husband's arm, she moved away.

A strange feeling began to come over Aunt Emmeline, a longing for Alfred. But Alfred was in the Isle of Wight; she moved towards the door.

A little man with a camera burst in through it, blocking her exit. "Is this the house?" he said abruptly. "This where the Spanish dancer lives—the one who's making a come-back after ten years?" Before Aunt Emmeline could answer him he turned and looked out into the hall.

An astonishing procession was coming down the stairs. First came a triumphant girl with flashing eyes and black, floating hair, then a round little man with equally black eyes, who was beaming with pride. Between them, fragile and birdlike, draped in a bright shawl and with her gleaming, satin-dark hair piled high, glided La Golondrina.

The little man held up his hand. "Announce, please!" he said. "I have announce to make. La Golondrina—" bowing profoundly, he turned and kissed her hand—"and I, Enrico Ribera, we get married, we go back to Spain!"

As the cameras clicked once more and the congratulations broke out, Emmeline saw the dark girl rush away from the group and over to Martin.

"And Mr. Pollard's going to paint her portrait!" she cried, "and it's sure to be in the Academy, and we are going to Spain for just a little while, a month or two, and then we shall come back—for my education," she explained, "and we must still live here—I shall insist!"

And as the babble of questions and congratulations swelled once more, a drab, deflated little woman, clutching a string-bag, completely unnoticed by anyone and longing now only for her kindly husband, escaped and made her way back to the bus.

At last they all went. The Spaniards in a flurry of flowers and protestations went off to dine at a restaurant which Enrico promised to La Golondrina would be perfectly safe—for was it not run by a member of his own family?—and the others slipped back to their flats. Lord Simon went off to his boys' club, and the two Johns returned in their car to the studio and from there to another restaurant to celebrate: John Pollard full of visions of La Golondrina's portrait, which should liberate him from fat women forever, and John Pim full of satisfaction at the beauty of Songberd's Grove. For the last time, as they left, Martin shook his head.

All of them had wanted him to go with them, Geneva and the two Johns to their restaurants, Lord Simon to his club. The Roseggs had begged the Singers to come upstairs to a feast of veal and noodles. Tom Triplett had mentioned that this evening he happened to have plenty of steak. But home was home and tonight there was cottage pie.

As the last person vanished and Martin was left standing in the empty row, he looked up at the face of Nicholas Songberd above the door. All round him the paint was shining; beneath was the bright red door. To one side was the pale-blue plaque of honour, and inside, in the house which Nicholas Songberd had built, were Martin's parents, happy and at their ease. Out through the window, from the wireless, the strains of a trumpet stole forth. Stone face and boy's face looked into each other's; to both it seemed a job well done.

Martin heaved a deep sigh of relief. So that was that. Now he could get on with the things that he really wanted to do.